THE FAIRY GODMOTHER

THE FAIRY GODMOTHER

Charles Baxter Clement

Caroline House Publishers Inc.

AURORA, IL

Copies of this book may be purchased from the publisher for $8.95. All inquiries and catalog requests should be addressed to Caroline House Publishers, Inc., 920 West Industrial Drive, Aurora, Illinois 60506. Phone 312-897-2050.

ISBN: 0-89803-035-8

LIBRARY OF CONGRESS
CATALOG CARD NO.: 80-29340

For Little Charlie
and the girls

Chapter 1

THE WAITER FINALLY brought our drinks, which made me feel better. I was annoyed because Janet was staring at the boy in the bikini. "Boy" is probably the wrong word. He was built like a horse, and apparently hung like one too. I don't know why that bothered me. I wasn't particularly the jealous type. And I had always felt I was pretty attractive to the ladies, even having just crossed the magic forty marker. I guess it was a question of loyalty—after all we had been through lately.

Fortunately she wasn't the only one staring at him. Half the old biddies at the beach bar were risking slipped discs pretending they were interested in the scuba-diving demonstration. The rich are so sad when it comes to sex. They seem to deny themselves everything that isn't their sole privilege.

I watched as her eyes flickered in confusion between the shiny tanks he was strapping to his back and his crotch. She had such magnificent eyes. They were very large, and so clear they were light gray. They were like every part of her physique. At the very peak of a lush late-twenties perfection. Tall, slender, and firm. Breasts like cantaloupes. An ass like soft marble. I took a long drink from my Bloody Mary.

There's nothing wrong with it, I reasoned with myself.

Frankly she ought to be attracted to him instead of me. That seems to be what nature intends. But maybe not. Perhaps nature gives youth its appeal not to attract pollen, but to attract protection. Rich old bastards like myself.

And that's what I was. I was a very rich man. Or at least I would be within a matter of hours. For, you see, I was the recipient of a most unusual beneficence. One so unusual I'm almost hesitant to discuss it. Far different from your run-of-the-mill, poor-boy-made-millionaire-industrialist. Or the Rockefeller nephew who patiently accepts his due at age twenty-one. No, this one was really different. One which will try your credulity. Unless you should, in the words of our Lord, become as little children.

Speaking of innocence, I remember Janet then turned toward me and said, "I want lunch."

Her golden hair glistened like a halo. It was fifty-fifty whether it was I or her stomach that took her mind from the boy's thighs, but I didn't care. It set my mind at ease.

"I'm waiting for a message," I replied.

"We can wait for it at the table, can't we?" she argued. "Just tell them you're expecting a telephone call."

"It may not be a telephone call," I said. "Someone is trying to reach me. That's all I know."

"Well, they know you're here at the resort," she said, standing. "They can find us as easily in the restaurant as on the terrace."

Taken by her logic, I drained the remainder of the Bloody Mary and stood. She proceeded toward the restaurant, but not before first exchanging a glance with the scuba diver.

It must have had some effect, since the tanks on his back suddenly fell to the floor with a bang. In the restaurant we took a seat with an ocean view. Janet ordered white wine on the rocks, while I chose another Bloody. Both of us then sat mesmerized by the reflections from the gemlike Caribbean waters.

When the waiter arrived with the drinks, I ordered eggs Benedict, and she chose seafood salad. Again our attention returned to our drinks and to the almost fairyland environment. I had been nervous all morning. I had even waked at five o'clock. But now, for some reason, I felt calmed. Perhaps it was Janet, with her simpler, pleasant mind. Or even the sea, which was so immense and calm. But, for some reason, I now felt no urgency. I felt certain that everything would go all right.

Soon the food arrived. There was something about the eggs that disturbed my appetite. They were small and somewhat overcooked. And the yokes were too yellow. Almost orange. Surely everything will go well, I told myself. It must. Everything is so well counterbalanced.

"I want to try the scuba diving," Janet announced, tearing off a corner of her roll. "It's something I've always wanted to do."

"Always since fifteen minutes ago," I muttered, experiencing a sinking feeling. She had never done anything like this before. Maybe she was getting tired of me.

"We're not doing anything, until I hear from my friend," I insisted. "This is the only *business* I'm doing down here, and you must cooperate."

(3

"Well, later this afternoon," she shrugged. "There's no big rush."

Suddenly I heard my name paged, and I jumped. I signaled the waiter and gave him my name. While he was gone, my stomach cramped, and I could feel my whole body shake. And it wasn't just the money, although that was enough to make a monk squirm. It was something else. Something I had felt all morning, but couldn't define. And then it struck me. I was finally going to meet Her. After all those months of work and fear and wonder, I was going to meet Her. For a moment I couldn't decide which was more important.

The waiter returned shortly and announced my taxi had arrived. I assured him I hadn't ordered a taxi, but that I was expecting a telephone call or perhaps a telegram. No, he replied, the driver was ready to take me to the town. Annoyed at his insistence, I repeated huffily that I hadn't ordered the taxi and wasn't about to leave. Even Janet piped in with a "That's absurd."

Just as the waiter turned to leave, I leaped for his sleeve. "Let me talk with the driver," I gasped. When I found the driver standing next to his automobile, I asked him where we were going. "To the Winterthur Bank," he replied with suspicion. "Just like you instructed on the telephone this morning."

"Fine, fine," I replied, hearing the name. The ol' Gal had done it. It was about to happen. The end was beginning.

I returned to the table to tell Janet I was leaving and that I would be back sometime in the afternoon. She said she wanted to shop in town and was coming along. I told her that was impossible, and besides—and this *hurt*—she wanted to go scuba diving.

I left Janet fluffing her soft golden tresses and headed toward the taxi. My mind raced, struggling to remember if there were anything I should take with me. But that was the bizarre feature of this circumstance. All I needed was myself. My face and my signature. It's the way all business should be conducted. The way the rich have always had it. With very little "luggage."

And then a pleasing prospect offered itself, as I hustled along the terrace. My eye was drawn toward the small dock in the bay, and there I saw the scuba diver standing at the helm of his speedboat. He was starting his engines, a small black dock boy holding his bowline. "Oh, shame of shames!" I sang, as I wound my way through the small tables in the bar. Bikini boy's already got a scuba party, and poor Janet's going to have to stay at home. He'd cry if he knew what he was missing. Hell, he'd probably quit his job. But who said life was fair? If it were, most of us couldn't make a living, much less get laid.

And I started to run. I hadn't run hard for years, except playing tennis or trying to catch a train. And it felt good. I was on my way to Elysium. And I was going to meet Her.

Chapter 2

LIFE WASN'T ALWAYS this zany. In fact, most of it had been spent at the other end of the spectrum. I grew up in Detroit—Grosse Pointe, to be exact. My father was an executive with the Ford Motor Company, and we had a pleasant enough life. He got ccut from the varsity in his early fifties, so we never made it to the top floor. But there was always enough bread for the finer things in life. I went to Grosse Pointe Country Day. I couldn't get into Princeton, so I went to Penn. I was a pretty good student, though, and was able to get an MBA from Wharton. I married a gal from Swarthmore my last year in Philadelphia.

My ambition in life was to be an entrepreneur. You know, get a great Western idea, struggle to find the capital—the wife tutoring in French to meet the mortgage payments—and finally achieve Nirvana in the form of some new Holiday Inns or Federal Express. But, unfortunately, my father cut me off at graduation, and I needed a job. Contrary to popular belief, the old MBA was no ticket to fifty grand a year. In fact, the only job I could get was with a Wall Street bond firm hustling municipals. It paid a draw of $750 a month, plus commissions.

So I started selling bonds. Selling was something new to me. If you were from Grosse Point and a frat boy at Penn, the only selling you did was in the back seat of a car, so things were pretty rough at first. But the little lady wanted to Junior League our stay in New York and I wanted to try all the big-time pleasures. So I had to get off my ass and talk the hicks in Indiana into buying my big-city paper. It was a real eye-opener.

It is certain that nothing is what it seems. And that is certainly true for the bond business. For obvious reasons everyone connected with the industry—the business and government leaders issuing the bonds, the dealers and salesmen selling them, and the fund managers at banks and insurance companies buying them—wants the public to have the right impression of what's going on. After all, it's the public's money they're playing with, and in most cases they're getting paid a fortune to do it.

The first impression they want to create is that the entire industry is the very bastion of conservatism. That's why they all wear those dark pin-stripe suits. The suits are supposed to conjure up visions of the Inquisition. And that's why most firms have oak-paneled offices. You're supposed to believe they've been there since Henry VIII cut off his first head. The truth, of course, is far removed. Most of these people (a) drink far too much, (b) cheat on their wives, and (c) are here today and gone tomorrow. In fact, most of them tend toward the raunchier side of the middle-class miasma.

The second great impression they promote is that they are very wise and intelligent. And this is perhaps the cruelest hypocrisy. For most of them are splendidly mediocre, having usually obtained their positions through luck, family, or deception, meaning they were able to hide their stupidity. They barely understand what they're doing, but make up for it through bluff and hustle.

But, regardless, there they all are in the canyons of Wall Street, jealously guarding what must be the best kept secret in Christendom.

I prefer to remember myself as something of an exception to the truths stated above. I was certainly no genius. I guess my IQ was somewhere in the mid-120s. But I always had savvy. At least I learned early that silence promotes the impression of depth. And I wasn't all that rambunctious. In fact, the first ten years in New York were spent pursuing the social ideals of our parents. We always lived in the nicest neighborhood my income could afford. We strove to meet other young couples of our rank and odor, unless they were unusually talented or successful. We dressed well, practiced our wines, and endured a number of operas and symphony concerts. It was dull, but we didn't really know it. And it was certainly a tremendous waste of time.

Life at the office was a little more interesting. After a year or so, I had become a pretty good salesman. Commissions in those days were nothing like today, but I was doing pretty well. In fact, I switched firms a couple of times, each switch bringing in a little more money. I had found out that the best way to sell some fund manager was to get to be his friend. Now, I know that sounds awful, but it's the truth. Puff him up, get him drunk, show him a good time. And when he was having troubles with the wife, always side with the wife. That type always goes back to the wife. And then he thinks you're a really decent fellow.

Another trick I used was to advise my customers—most salesmen use the word "client"—on where the markets were headed. That means whether bond prices were going up or down. Now, I didn't know where they were going, but I could gather all the bullshit in the newspapers and from the coffee drinkers around the office. The key was to tell the customer everything you knew without ever really making a suggestion. That means saying things like "I sure wouldn't want to be 'long' this market." Which means I hadn't recommended he go short, but if he should make money, I want part of the credit. Or "I like being 'short,' but I would never vote against you." That way, if I'm right, he thinks I'm a genius, and if he's right, I puff his ego.

Well, enough customers had commented about my market opinion that one day the general manager of our operation asked me into his office and offered me a job as an assistant trader for the firm. Now a "trader" is a different animal in the bond business. He's the guy who neither spins nor toils. He just sits there and *thinks*. It's the ultimate situation.

The trader's supposed to tell the salesmen where the market's going, so they can sell the information, as well as the bonds. He's also supposed to create inventory for the salesmen. In other words, if a salesman comes in and says his customer wants ten million of a certain bond, the trader's supposed to be able to get it at a cheaper price. And then, he's supposed to trade the house account. Now, this is something rarely talked about. After all, those old "bastions of conservatism" aren't supposed to be speculators. But the truth is, they are. And it's a major source of their income. Or losses.

And who would pass up such an opportunity? After all, the big bond house is at the very center of the market. Hell, they *create* the market. And with a little cooperation from the dozen or so other houses. . . . But we mustn't even consider the unspeakable.

So at age thirty I was an assistant trader at a major bond house. It was an easy enough job. The higher-ups wanted to make all the decisions anyway, so I just kissed their asses and made a nice living. And the money was pretty good too. We all got bonuses based on the trading gains. It was sort of heads I win, tails you lose. After all, it wasn't our money. And with a lot of "staying power," any loss would eventually become a winner.

So I would get to the office about nine, send the secretary out for coffee and Danish, and read the *Wall Street Journal*. The *Journal* really did most of the work. Imagine the job if those folks didn't gather all the information every morning? About nine-thirty one of the senior guys would get on the loudspeaker and disperse his pearls amongst us swine. Of course, all he was doing was repeating what we had all just read in the *Wall Street Journal*, along with some goodies he'd pick up from buddies at other bond houses. You see, traders are a class unto themselves, like medieval knights or Renaissance castratti. And their first loyalty is always to their own kind. They're always giving away secrets and otherwise helping the competition because they may need the same help some day. And, of course, God help the poor bastard who doesn't play the game. They'd bury him.

Then I would spend the rest of the morning talking with the salesmen, buying or selling bonds with customers or others, sometimes swapping bonds, if there was a profit in it. It was really quite pleasant, as long as you never stuck your neck out. About twelve-thirty, the traders would usually repair to a local restaurant and spend a couple of hours drinking and listening to the head guys beat their chests and repeat tales of conquest and cunning. There's supposed to be a lot of ego tied up with the business. I guess it shows you're tough and competitive.

Afternoons were different. Naturally the traders didn't want to have to work every afternoon—they're really big on squash. So for some strange reason, markets were always slower in the afternoon, and you could leave at least a couple times a week to play or shop.

As I say, it was a real nice way to make a living. And I've always wondered why everybody else doesn't do the same thing. I guess it *is* the best kept secret in the world.

This went on for three or four years, and they kept gradually moving me up. Each time I got a little bit better deal, but the wife had no problem disposing of the extra money. But then a couple of years ago something happened which almost ruined the whole thing. Two of the head guys quit, and a third died in a boating accident. To make things worse, the fellow just ahead of me decided to return to sales.

Well, you can guess what happened. Within a week I was made chief trader for the firm. I thought the world had come to an end. Of course, there was more money—a lot more. But—for God's sake—I didn't know what the hell I was doing! I had to use every trick I knew to appear like a genius. And naturally the traders from other houses made me look good. Helping the "new boy" out, you know.

Fortunately everything worked out, and soon I was the new guru of the house. And, contrary to what I had always feared, I soon rather liked the job. The money was fabulous. They were paying close to a hundred and eighty a year, plus all sorts of perks. The trading was easy. Just read the *Wall Street Journal*, talk with all your buddies and spend a couple of hours on Sunday putting it all together. After all, when all the gurus agree, where else is the market going. We *are* the market.

And I really liked the status the position gave me. All the other executives used to line up to go to lunch with me. The secretaries would flirt openly—more of that later—and even the customers used to send *me* Christmas presents. It was a good deal, and naturally it went to my head a little bit. I began buying European suits and took up a pipe. I also allowed a slight affectation to slip into my speech patterns. It had a touch of Boston and a smattering of Eastern Shore. It certainly had nothing to do with Detroit. I was also acquiring a little arrogance. After all, I was directing the financial course of the Western world. I was quoted in *Barron's*. I was important!

But then one day all that changed. In fact, my whole life changed. From its very top to bottom. I had always heard that that could happen to someone, but I never dreamed it would happen to me. And it was all because of Her. She stepped in, waved Her wand, so to speak, and made me into a different person. And it happened quite that simply.

Chapter 3

I SUPPOSE I SHOULD say something about my wife. I truly can't remember when it started going wrong. I was very much in love when we got married. I would rush home every afternoon simply to be with her. And the lovemaking—while not particularly athletic—was sublime.

And I think she was in love with me, although in retrospect she even then seemed preoccupied with *organizing* our lives. But we used to like to snuggle in front of the television and hold hands while shopping. We used to get senseless fits of giggles in strange places, such as weddings or at the movies or in front of our parents. I thought it was great fun and never dreamed it would get anything but better.

But, alas, it changed. And some eighteen years later it had become a nightmare—at least for me. In short, she, my lovely bride, had become—and again, I can't tell you why—a small-minded, selfish, social-conscious, middle-aged bitch.

I know that seems harsh, but I felt I was living with a stranger, someone I'd barely met. There were times when I felt like introducing myself, saying, "Hey, babe, it's me, ol' Bobby! Let's sit down and smooch or have a beer or play tennis or cook spaghetti, like in the old days." But I couldn't even do that. She would have accused me of drinking too much at lunch.

No, it had become a world of manners. Of manners and *things*. The right apartment, the right friends, the fur coats—all that hogwash even our parents took with a grain of salt. It was as if we were aspiring to be Queen Elizabeth III. I can't understand it and have great difficulty explaining it.

Perhaps it was my fault—who knows? But I can't think of one instance where I *changed*. Where I stopped being attentive or generous or fun. Oh, I played a little more squash and went out a few more nights than before. But I always looked to her for the tone in the marriage. And she never really complained. All I can say is that she kept her figure, but lost her sense of humor.

And she was the mother of my two sons. And I did love my sons. Although they were the strangest two kids I've ever known. I mean, I spent every free hour for almost fifteen years playing or working with them. And I think it did some good. One of them had just started at Duke, and the other was at Lawrenceville. But it's as if I had never met them, the older they got. And it's not like the old, traditional Generation Gap. These kids were really weird. They made good grades, but they studied things like ancient botany and middle Hebrew. What's wrong with European History 201?

And they *lived* off marijuana. They even grew the damned stuff on the terrace. It upset me at first, but all our friends assured us it did more harm than good to fight it. It sure calmed 'em down—for whatever that's worth. It was all very confusing.

By the time the big promotion came, I had already had my second affair, you might call it. Hell, they were nothing but embarrassing one-night stands with gals in the office. I was too awkward and frightened to have made them much better. I blamed it on the age-status difference. But in truth I was just green.

It took Her to do it. To rearrange my life. To set me free from my condition. And ironically it happened the day after I had to manipulate the wife out of her first suspicion.

It was a morning like any other. I had arrived at the office with a benign hangover—we had been to a dinner party given by the Women's Board of Unwed Mothers or some such cabal. The secretary—God bless her soul—saw the telltale signs and ushered in the coffee and Danish. I shut the door—I now had a private office—and placed my face on the desktop. I felt like hell. It was what I call a nauseous-throbber. Usually produced by excellent Russian vodka mixed with superb Italian vermouth.

Finally I raised my head and began sipping the coffee. I kept telling myself that this too would pass. That within hours, if not days, I would feel whole again. That nothing would hurt. I even found courage to open the *Journal*.

My eyes became fixed on an article about the modern maple syrup industry in Vermont. I wasn't really reading the article and I wasn't thinking about anything else. My eyes just seemed to stick there. Then the phone rang. And it took me several seconds to discover the source of the pain. I didn't want to talk with anyone, but I had to do something to stop the sound. I lifted the receiver.

And that's when I first heard the voice. High-pitched, nasal to the point of whiny, broken by rapid modulations. It was a horrible sound. One which made my flesh crawl. Not because of its animal tones, but because I knew it was human. And I had never met another human—one on one—who sounded that grotesque.

"Mis-ter Reed?" the voice asked. "Is that you?"

At first I couldn't answer. I was certain the wages of sin were upon me and that any moment other, more horrible hallucinations would spring forth.

"*Mis-ter Reed?*" it shrilled. "Are you there?"

My mind was total confusion. But just in the event it was our honorable chairman, I replied weakly, "Yes, it is. Who's calling?"

"Oh, it's an old friend," the voice whined. "A very old friend."

"What do you want, old friend?" I mumbled, figuring it was some idiot customer who hadn't sobered up from the night before.

"I want an *ap-point-ment*," it said slowly, the sound sending revulsion through my already tortured midsection.

I was stymied. I had no idea who was speaking. And I didn't know what to say next. My only desire was to hang up the phone and return to the desktop.

"May I ask who this is?" I asked. "I'm really quite busy."

"We need to meet," the voice replied softly, its pitch lowering.

"Please come by the office," I murmured, my head beginning to throb. "I'm free most anytime this week."

There was a long pause. For one gorgeous moment I thought perhaps it had hung up.

"Do you mind telling me who's calling?" I asked, growing impatient. "I'm really quite busy."

"I want to meet you at the Port Authority," the voice hissed slowly.

"Aw, come on," I moaned. "Who the hell is this?"

Well, it hung up without a further word, which really pissed me off. It was obviously a crank call, but it's always irritating when someone hangs up on you. I re-placed my head on the desk, vowing to remind the secretary to get names before sending calls in.

Somehow I survived the morning. We had just participated in a big government note auction and I had to support the market so the salesmen could sell the crap. That meant making all sorts of false bids in other issues to make the unwashed think prices were going up.

At lunch I went to Delmonico's with a stock analyst buddy who I knew would be supportive vis-à-vis the hangover. A couple of gimlets helped immensely, and I was able to return to the office for another hour or so. At three I announced I had a meeting at one of the banks and left. I headed straight toward the Racquet Club, where I fell into a long, stinging, and delicious steambath before showering and hitting the "sleep room." At about five I woke and went down to the bar. A couple of tall Scotch and sodas made me feel almost normal. At least it gave me enough courage to face Godzilla.

You see, my wife objected to my getting drunk at her soirees. Well, it's not my getting drunk so much as my telling some old biddie to go to hell or my falling asleep at the dinner table. But I guess I couldn't blame her. She liked to pretend I was the Christian answer to the Rothschilds, while I preferred to see myself as a cross between Mick Jagger and Jimmy Connors.

I knew she'd be particularly uninteresting that certain evening, since I had been exceptionally amusing the night before—like biting some old lady on the ass while waiting for our cars. But there was nothing I could do. I had to face it like a man. It was like getting the old prostate checked.

It was as bad as I had anticipated. It started out as the silent treatment—Oh, blessed wonder!—but then quickly degenerated into the primordial scream. Immediately the headache, the painful stomach, and the shakes returned to life. I retreated to the wet bar in the library.

"It was the most dis*gusting* display I've seen from you to date," she thundered, her rich Main Line accent rising to its upperest.

"I did-dent bite the lady, Terry," I answered as firmly as I could. "I was picking up the car keys."

"I saw you, Bob, so please don't lie to me," she argued. "I saw the mouth open and the teeth *close*."

This last word was said rather viciously. I knew she had me. You see, I *had* bitten the lady on the ass.

"Perhaps she enjoyed it," I shrugged, turning and retreating toward the living room.

"Enjoyed it?" Terry roared. "The . . . the chairman of the New York Metropolitan Benefit Council? Mrs. Twingingham could possibly have *enjoyed* . . . saliva . . . and teeth marks on her Halston gown? You . . . you are . . . *gross*."

"No, I meant . . . in a . . . playful way," I mumbled, looking for the newspaper.

"*You*," she baritoned, "are truly repulsive at moments like this. And you're going to ruin my whole career in New York."

"Career?" I asked, hoping to trip her up a bit. "What career is that?"

She paused, glancing down at her trim beige suitcoat before patting at the buttons. Her hair looked pretty pulled back and out, even if it was rather stiff.

"No, I'm serious," I said, placing my drink on the fireplace mantel. "What career?"

"You have *never*," she began calmly, yet forcefully, "ever known or appreciated what I have done for this family or for you or your career."

She kept it up for the better part of thirty minutes, so I decided it was time to turn to Plan D. You see, Plan A was to placate—"Terry, I'm sorry, and I'll never do it again." Plan B was to argue—"I did *not* bite the lady on the ass. I simply bent over to pick up the car keys." Plan C was the male version of the silent treatment, ofttimes followed by a night at the club. But Plan *D*. That was something else. A tactic used in only those rarest and most pressing circumstances. And only if you were absolutely sure it would work.

Right in the midst of one of her shrillest bleats I walked to the piano stool, stepped up, and looked around. The sound stopped. I then proceeded higher, until I was standing full square on top of the piano. I knew it would hold me because I tested it one night. I then turned toward her opened mouth and shouted, "Shut the fuck up or I'll throw the Meissen goblets down twenty-two stories!"

I then returned to the floor, walked passed a face Michelangelo could have used for the *Pietà*, and went to my room—we now had separate rooms. I took off all my clothes and walked back through the living room to the library. I grabbed the ice bucket and a bottle of Scotch. Tears were streaming down her face as I turned to smile good night. I knew that would be the last of it for the evening. The only risk would be whether she would leave for her mother's. I wasn't too worried about that. Since the kids had gone off to school, she knew the mother-trip was now something of a vacation for me.

I threw open the covers, mixed a stiff drink, and crawled inside with a new book by Walker Percy. I reached toward the night table and tuned to a classical music station. My friend, it had all the makings of a very nice hangover evening. As Father always said, "Make stepping stones out of stumbling blocks."

The telephone rang, and I had to decide whether to answer it or not. If it were for Terry, I could simply tell the party to ring again until she answered. But if it were for me—and *she* answered—she would probably tell them I had left for Afghanistan. So I lifted the receiver. And my entire body chilled.

Chapter 4

PHYSICAL FEAR IS a humiliating emotion. It makes one feel truly unimportant. It's a reminder, I suppose, of our original purpose on earth. And I was genuinely afraid when I heard the sound. Immediately I knew it was no friend. A friend wouldn't persist. And I knew it was someone abnormal. For who could make those sounds—create those fears in another—without living beyond self-revulsion.

Even though I felt secure in the apartment, I felt horribly threatened by the fact it was on the telephone. It was almost as if it could touch me. It knew my name and address. My place of work. Which meant it must have watched me for some time. Before I could even answer, it began telling me my age, my father's full name, the birth dates of my children, the color of my wife's eyes. It dropped them out slowly, often with a slight giggle.

And then I knew. It came to me immediately. This sickie had kidnapped one of the boys. This is how it happens. Place that essential sickening fear in the parents. Get them in the palm of the hand. And then *squeeze*.

"What do you want?" I finally gasped, not wanting to alert Janet.

"I want to meet," it said. "And very soon."

"Well, let me tell you this," I found myself saying rapidly.

"This whole thing can be handled quite amicably. You just relax. You yourself have nothing to fear so long as you . . . you are . . . *nice.*"

There was a long pause, during which my heart sank. Perhaps I had upset it. Perhaps it was so upset, it was going to punish one of the boys. I felt like crying out. I had to do something!

"I think. . . ," it quaked, "I think you have the, uh, wrong impression, Mr. Reed."

"What do you mean?" I asked.

Again there was a long pause, during which I could feel my heart pound.

"Do you have a pencil, Mr. Reed?" it asked rather pleasantly.

My spirits plunged as I tore from the bed and began ransacking the bureau top. It wanted to tell me where to deliver the money! I returned to the phone, watching my hands spasm.

"Yes," I said hoarsely. "I'm here."

It cleared its throat dramatically and then recited the following.

"M-I will be down three-point-four billion; M-2 will be down two-point-eight billion; and M-3 will be down two-point-seven-five billion."

And with that, it hung up.

I remained seated on the bed, my thoughts colliding. I rose—perhaps to go to Terry—but then sat back down. I grabbed the glass and drained it, then shook my head, trying to collect myself. I had never been so confused.

I quickly decided there had been no kidnapping, although a dull doubt remained. Why the grotesque voice, the gathering of information? The money supply figures? It didn't make sense.

Again I rose. Maybe Terry could explain it. But I decided against that. It would make her hysterical. Perhaps for days. So I sat down to call the boys, just to be sure they were safe. But, no, I was sure there was no kidnapping. But why was it calling *me*? What did it want from *me*?

I poured another drink and emptied half the glass. Perhaps it *was* simply a crank. Some seedy nut in the Bronx who'd created a new formula for predicting money supply. But why wouldn't he come to the office? Or write a book?

I finished the rest of the glass and settled back into bed. Surprisingly, I was able to get into the new book, with only occasional thoughts about the telephone calls. An hour and two glasses later I flicked off the light and turned to sleep. Somebody at the office will figure it out, I told myself. Besides, it'll make a great story. The Great Money Supply Monster. It'll add to my legend.

The next morning I felt like a million dollars. I even shaved with my straight razor. Terry had returned to the silent treatment, so I had to fix my own breakfast. I hadn't thought about the telephone calls until I was gathering my change on top of the bureau. There I spied the figures that I had written down and shoved them into my pocket. They would be part of the story. Besides it was Thursday, and the money supply figures would be announced at four o'clock. We could see if the nut were on to something.

When I arrived at the office I barely had time to take off my coat. The Treasury was about to announce a refunding at ten o'clock, and the President was speaking on a tax package at noon. The Street was calling money supply sharply higher, and there had been a bomb threat at the New York Stock Exchange. Markets were heavy and volatile. The place was going wild.

I got on the intercom and broadcast in my most distant and eccentric baritone, occasionally sucking on a pipe which I kept just for those occasions. I instructed the lads to trade from the long position. The refunding would be large, but would be concentrated in short-term instruments. Higher money was already in the market, and the President—according to my sources—wasn't going to scare anyone. In other words, buy the dips and sell the rallies.

My instructions turned out to be good, and the firm did exceptionally well. Even more importantly, the individuals had a good day, and I was once again the king of kings. I even got a call from the chairman. He just wanted to know what was happening. Actually he wanted to know if we were right or wrong. He knew the truth about traders, you see. He used to be one.

Well, I stayed in my office until about noon. I wanted the troops to be well soaked in blood before the review. And when I flung open the door, a veritable chorus of cheers erupted. I then walked with Caesar and Bonaparte and the great Robert E. A couple of the older secretaries even stood.

In my euphoria I accepted an invitation for lunch from one of our better young salesmen. He had a group of executives from a large Midwest pension fund in town and wanted to impress them. After Terry's performance, I was in the mood for a little adulation, so I accepted.

It took some time to tidy up, so we got a late start. The salesman pulled out all the stops and took his turkeys to the Four Seasons. We arrived at about two-thirty and immediately plunged into the martinis. I was at my wittiest and most erudite. I recounted tales about days at Wharton and awed them with a glimpse at my spiritual life. I told a couple of jokes, ordered my lunch in Country Day French, and otherwise lay back to enjoy the fruits of my station.

Shortly before four o'clock we found ourselves all huddled over Remy Martins. I was whispering the account of the travails of a prominent trader at the competition who had been seen at a sadomasochist gay bar. Just as I got to the good part one of the hicks jumped back and said, "My God! Money figures are announced in five minutes!"

It really upset the guru to be interrupted in such rude fashion, so I leaned back and swirled my cognac. "What's the figure going to be?" one of the customers asked me, himself insensitive to the insult. I paused, letting the luscious liquid coat the sides of the snifter. Then—for reasons I still can't fathom—I reached into my pocket and produced the scribblings from the night before. It was an insane thing to do. After all, the ravings of a lunatic are not exactly the stuff one feeds to customers.

"M-1 will be down three-point-four billion," I intoned. "M-2 will be down two-point-eight billion; and M-3 will be down two-point-seven-five billion." They were aghast.

"That's impossible!" gasped the fat one. "You yourself said it would be up this morning on the intercom."

"One doesn't *always* tell the truth," I resonated quietly into my glass. "Besides, in trading the only important factor is what everyone else thinks."

"I'm going to call the office," the youngster announced before leaping from his seat.

With a little urging I went back to the story of the trader caught in the gay bar. But once again—just as I got to the funny part—the young bastard returned breathless to the table and interrupted me. This time I started to tell him to shut his silly mouth.

"What were your figures?" he shouted.

"What figures?" I asked with obvious pique.

"The *money* figures," he replied. "The ones you just read."

"Well, let me see," I answered, hoping they weren't too ridiculous. "M-1 down three-point-four billion; M-2 down two-point-eight; and M-3 down two-point-seven-five."

"Impossible!" the kid shouted. "It's impossible! Those are the exact figures!"

"Let me see," the fat one exclaimed, grabbing the sheet from the boy. "By God, it is! They're exactly the same! That's impossible!"

Everyone at the table stared at me with mouths agape.

I myself had the presence to leave mine shut. I was so stunned, all I could think to do was to raise the snifter to take another petite sip. I neither heard the hosannas nor saw the young fellow fall to one knee.

You see, the figures were exactly the same. And that, simply put, is impossible.

Chapter 5

NOW, LET ME EXPLAIN to you what this money supply stuff is all about. A bunch of economists who work for the government have come to the brilliant conclusion that the more money people have, the more they spend. For this we need a government? And these same bureaucrats also feel that the more we spend, the faster we fuel inflation. So whenever they think there's too much money around, they raise our taxes—nice trick, eh?—or cut off our credit by raising interest rates, or both.

Well, to find out how much money's around, the Federal Reserve Bank—the government's banker, you might say—compiles a weekly figure taken from deposit records throughout the country. For instance M-1—the M stands for money—constitutes the folding money and coins in circulation, plus demand deposits, like personal checking accounts. M-2 includes all of that, but also certain time deposits, like certificates of deposit. The third category includes just about every type of money and credit. They use different categories because they reflect different areas of the economy, such as consumer spending or business spending.

Well, all of this is very dull, but it's also very important to bond traders. The Federal Reserve Bank, you see, can raise or lower interest rates charged by banks almost at will. And when interest rates change, the prices of bonds change.

I won't bore you with any more details, but the money supply figures were the most important feature to my work. If the supply of money goes up, the price of bonds usually goes down. And vice versa.

The figures are all gathered by the Federal Reserve Bank branch in New York City. I guess it's because New York has the best restaurants. They come together via a super-secret communications network located—according to rumor—in a room with no windows. It would be awfully simple for an informer to raise or lower a window shade, you see.

Regardless, the figures are so important that only a precious few people—maybe four or five—should know them before the release. And many, many people watch those few. As I said, it's *impossible* to know them. It's like state secrets. It's impossible!

I guess that's why I feigned the headache—we geniuses are prone to headaches, you know—and left the restaurant almost immediately. I was half drunk, but that wasn't the real problem. And all the hoopla from the guys at the table didn't bother me. The truth is I was staggered. The weirdo had scared me with the phone calls, but now he had done the impossible. Was it just a lucky guess? After all, a guess is at least possible! Theoretically.

And that raised the possibility of an inside man. But that too was impossible. They must watch those people like hawks. And how could an intelligent economist sound like that? Behave like that?

I decided to walk up Park Avenue. The January air was whipping down the alley, and it felt good. I decided I wasn't going to worry about it. I had time. It would all come clear in the end. Hell, I was over forty, old enough to take things in stride. I would rely on my experience which taught me there is an answer to everything. It didn't work.

I stepped into the Racquet Club and headed toward the steam room. I avoided looking at people. I was afraid I would be tempted to discuss the situation, and they would think me nuts.

After I undressed I looked at myself in the mirror. That too was a confusing sight. I still, overall, looked pretty good. There was no bulge, no puffiness. In fact, the occasional pushups and situps had done a decent job. And the old member still stood out fairly straight. Not like most of my friends whose entire genitalia languored lost somewhere between their thighs. I looked alive. Perhaps appealing.

The steam was disappointing. It stung my skin, causing a restlessness. I showered and dressed hurriedly, then repaired to the bar. The bar was virtually empty. There were a couple of three-piece punks seated at a card table and an older man at the end of the bar whose conversation about the creation of the Union Pacific Railroad had driven me to distraction several months before. My God, I thought, why do snobs think they have to live in nineteenth-century England to be attractive?

I ordered a drink for nothing better to do. I was almost desperate for someone to talk with. I knew Terry would still be sharpening her knife, and there was no professional friend I could call. Something told me to keep my mouth shut. But there was always Janet.

It's time to come clean about Janet. I'll try to describe her characteristics in mixed order of chronology and importance. She was about five-ten. Blonde hair. Firm, large breasts. Lovely, small, tight waist. A well-rounded ass with two very long, soft legs attached thereto. She was a graduate of Smith College. An MBA from the University of Virginia. Three years experience as a clerk-typist in the Mergers and Acquisitions Department—followed by a very amusing EEOC suit—before becoming a $30,000 a year preferred-stock analyst at the firm. She had an efficiency in the East 60s, a cat named Puppet, and a Renault Le Car. Her folks lived in Tucson, Arizona, following early retirement from Consolidated Foods in Chicago. She had a brother at Arizona State on a football scholarship, and his twin sister was studying drama in Minneapolis. The twins, it seems, were something of a miscalculation.

She had a disarming smile. A lot of energy. Good taste in clothes—as do most girls that age, for some reason. A more than adequate disposition. And a good measure of ambition. She liked to make love, eat at good restaurants, and occasionally give back rubs.

We met at the office, while she was dating a kid who works for me. Our first date was to go see *Deep Throat*—she couldn't get the younger guy to take her. We had dinner a week later after a late office meeting. We made love one afternoon in her apartment some three weeks later. She knew I was married. We were trying to keep the thing on some sort of reasonable two-leaves-in-the-storm basis. It wasn't working. More of that later.

I thought I might still catch her at the office, so I asked for the telephone at the bar. Her secretary would have left sharply at 5:00, so I dialed the night number. I let it ring six or seven times, until finally she picked it up. She answered in a professional tone of voice—which was both pleasant and noncommittal and meant to placate both bosses and lovers.

"Whatcha doing?" I asked, a wave of security passing over me.

"Oh, hi," she purred. "Just finishing up stuff I've put off all day. You know I had that big Commonwealth Edison presentation today."

I marveled at the way she—as well as many of her sisters—could maintain such marvelous poise, after what must have been a very trying day. I mean, it's not trading bonds or anything truly trying, but it's still tougher than what those idiots at Colgate Palmolive do.

"Am I calling too late?" I asked, figuring I'd better try the defenseless routine, since it was so late.

"Too late for what?" she asked.

I was at a loss for words. I desperately needed to be with someone, and she was the best someone I knew. And whatever she had planned that night I wanted her to break. It wasn't just silly courting or even jealousy—we both knew she was dating other guys. Now that I discovered I wanted to be with someone—and she was the *only* someone—I couldn't take the risk of a turndown. It had to work. I was suddenly almost sickeningly tense.

"To give *me* a few minutes," I answered jovially.

"Well, I'm supposed to meet this jerk from Westinghouse for a drink," she replied laconically. "But that shouldn't last later than eight or so."

"Can you get out of it?" I asked, my hopes soaring.

"It's part of my *job*," she protested, letting the last word string out tantalizingly.

"I'll buy us a couple of two-pounders," I murmured. "It'll be so much you won't even get to the tail."

"Oooooh, that's the best part," she replied before bursting into laughter. "I'll tell you what! You get the lobster and a head of Romaine lettuce and go to the apartment. I'll take Bubble Butt to the bar downstairs and be finished by six-thirty."

"Blessed are you among women—" I started.

"Gotta run!" she shouted, then hung up.

I replaced the receiver and stared at the stolid bartender. I felt the luckiest of men. Despite the headache, the anxiety over the weirdo and the Terry-disaster, I felt relaxed and renewed. A young and beautiful girl liked me. She was going to break a date, so to speak, and have a quiet, intimate dinner with me. And following a most passionate and skillful lovemaking, we were going to lie next to each other naked. And while rubbing each other with moistened fingertips, I was going to spill out the problem. And she would understand and help me. And all would come clear, just as we curled together for a sleep of the innocents.

But, oh, I had to remember Terry. What would it be this time? Most stock excuses were out because I fully intended to spend the entire night with Janet. There was only one solution. I wouldn't call her at all. After the emotional brutalization I had suffered at her hands, I couldn't possibly face more. The excuse came. I had slunk to the Johnston's where poor George stayed up half the night listening to my besotted hysteria. That might even patch things up. I made a note to remind myself to forewarn poor George.

Taxis appeared difficult to come by, so I walked the several blocks to the store. I bought the lobsters, along with the lettuce and some special cheese, all the time humming the tune to "Solitaire's the Only Game in Town." Walking toward Janet's apartment I felt closer to her than ever before. The memory of her face, with its perfect skin and slightly sunken cheeks, conjured up fleeting thoughts of a more permanent union. But that was silly. We had known each other only for a few short months.

The doorman recognized me and tipped his hat as I proceeded to the elevator. That worried me a little bit. Suppose Terry hired a private detective? The doorman could ruin me. But why get paranoid? There were pleasanter things to consider at the moment. Inside the apartment I placed the food on the kitchen counter and turned to take off my coat. Just then the telephone rang.

I remember it just as if it had happened yesterday. I

seemed to walk in slow motion toward the telephone, having some sort of difficulty with my coat. It was Janet calling for some reason—perhaps to say Bubble Butt from Westinghouse was keeping her a little longer than expected. I remember lifting the receiver not yet having extricated my other arm from its sleeve.

"Hello, sweet thing," I whispered.

"*Sweet thing*!" it screamed.

My head went light, and I dropped to my knees. I began trembling visibly. I was going insane! My mind was going berserk! I was hallucinating! Oh, God, *help* me! I screamed silently.

"Oh, how nice, Mr. Reed," it shrilled. "I'm so glad we've reached a better understanding."

"Who *are* you?" I moaned. "What do you want?"

"I want to meet you, Mr. Reed," it replied, its voice sliding to the baritone. "We have many things to discuss."

"But what?" I asked weakly, for some reason ready to cry.

"What?" it asked, its voice returning to the feminine. "Didn't you like my figures?"

"Who are you?" I asked. "You work for the government? Who are you?"

There was a long pause, and I became afraid it had left the phone. I didn't want that. I wanted to find out. I wanted to end this sickening phantasmagoria.

"What's your name?" I pleaded. "Please! What the hell do you want?"

"I'm your . . . fairy godmother," it said slowly. "Yes,

that's what I am. Your *fairy godmother*. And I'm going to do nice things for you. As long as you're a good little boy."

"That doesn't make shit for sense, and you know it," I shouted, trying to shock the animal into some sort of reality. "We'll get along much better if you just act like a normal human being."

Again there was a long pause, during which my apprehension returned. I cleared my throat.

"Listen," I said reasonably. "We're either going to get one thing straight or else—"

It interrupted me with a long, screeching, high-pitched sound that turned the hairs on my neck electric. Jesus Christ, I was ready for anything.

"*You . . . will. . . ,*" it began, before apparently composing itself, "you will meet me next Wednesday . . . at ten o'clock . . . at the Port Authority . . . on the Main Concourse . . . in the men's toilet . . . last stall on the right."

It took me several seconds to understand what he had just said, and then I gasped. "You want *me* to meet *you* in a fucking public *bathroom*? Are you nuts or something? Listen—"

With that, it hung up.

Chapter 6

THE WORST PART of loneliness is not the damage to the self—that slow, painful deterioration of one's confidence that he's okay. One can counter that by making more money or going to a new beauty salon or putting together model airplanes. No, the real damage—the scar tissue—comes in the failure to conspire. For there are truly strength and solace in numbers.

For the next week I yearned for someone with whom I could discuss my situation. Janet was out of the question. By the time she returned to the apartment I was so unnerved I could barely get an erection. I was afraid she wouldn't believe me. That she would think I had gone insane. Or would suggest I call the police. Or tell my wife! Or report to my boss! I was a real mess, and the evening a total failure.

What did the thing want? Why did it keep calling me? I had already eliminated the kidnapping theory, but maybe it was some sex deviate. But why the money supply figures? Was that part of its ploy? And how did it know the figures? Was it just a lucky guess? It couldn't be anyone at the Fed. Can you imagine the chairman of the Federal Reserve talking on the telephone like that? But how else would the figures be known? A case of electronic espionage? A cleaning lady who's been to the Harvard Business School? No, it must have been a lucky guess. It's got to be within the realm of probability.

Well, going to meet the freak was out of the question. I already knew that. It did cross my mind, however, to send a young associate or alert the Treasury Department. But, my God, they'd have thought me absolutely certifiable.

Strangely enough, my relations with Terry improved dramatically. I guess she could sense I was behaving abnormally and associated that with fears of a mental breakdown. Regardless, during the following few days she made no outside engagements and was home every night with a good meal. Well . . . as good as she could radar. I was tempted a couple of times to tell her something was on my mind. But I figured I'd better let the sleeping dog lie. She'd want a fur coat out of anything less than cancer of the colon.

At work things weren't much better. I barely showed up Friday. When I did walk into the office, the whole place erupted into pandemonium. After all, Bernard Baruch himself had been reincarnated. I couldn't very well tell them the information had come from some obscene voice over the telephone, so I played Lord Byron and left with a wistful look in my eye. I'm sure they attributed that to the spiritual burdens of True Greatness.

The weekend was even worse. I watched some basketball at a neighbor's house Saturday afternoon, and even he could tell something was wrong. I kept asking which "down" it was. Sunday I must have walked fifteen miles before falling into a Scotch bottle about six o'clock. I read a few more pages from the book.

I didn't want to go to work Monday, but I could see no way out. The whole matter had become something of an embarrassment, and I felt myself a total fraud. If I did it once, they would expect me to do it again. I decided that for the next several weeks I would strictly run with the pack on money estimates. Then maybe they'd forget about it, yet perhaps retain a slight sense of awe at the one great event. I still wished it had never happened.

Sure enough, the entrance Monday into the office was painful. Even after the handshakes and jokes, I could feel the eyes turning, the hushed conversations. I wanted to stay in my cubicle with the door shut, but I figured it was wiser to mingle. That would make me appear much more human.

Tuesday was a little bit better. The absolute deference had died down at least. I went to lunch with a couple of the boys. We talked about the Knicks and the marvels of Ivy League basketball.

I left work early and went on a shopping spree. I wasn't much of a clothes hound, but something put me into the mood. Unfortunately, I bought a new suit, two new sports coats, several pairs of slacks, and about a dozen custom shirts. But, what the hell, I could afford it.

My spirits were so much better that after I arrived home, Terry found the nerve to announce we were going out to dinner with our neighbors, the Tomlinsons. No rest for the weary. I tried regaining my wistful look, but it was futile.

Besides ol' Tomlinson had a *very* attractive wife, and I knew I could spend a part of the evening deciphering the curves to her fanny.

We stepped next door for a drink about seven and began putting on our coats about eight. I was talking with Marv about the cost of playing golf in the New York area, when suddenly a screech erupted from the cloak room. It was Terry and Pat having a private laugh, but it was enough to start the shaking all over again. It sounded so much like the weirdo, the whole anxiety process began again. I was truly miserable.

I sat silently through the meal at Terry's favorite bistro around the corner from the apartment. I could tell Marv and Pat knew something was wrong. Terry was irritated and would express as much through an occasional glance or a specially pursed lip. All I could think about was whether or not I was going to meet the Thing. It was absolutely out of the question, but I couldn't *put* it out of the question.

We arrived home fairly early, and I went straight to bed. The minute the light went out, I seemed to be more awake than during the entire day. So I turned the light back on and tried to read. Every second sentence my thoughts would return to the problem. I was frantic. I took two Valiums.

What was wrong with my going? I finally asked myself. I can get someone to go with me—in case there's trouble. Regardless, the place is lousy with cops. So what if it's repulsive? One sees the grotesque every day on the streets of New York. It'll probably turn out to be some short-haired freak who's simply an embarrassment. Or at worst some withered professor who's convinced he'll corner the world.

Somewhere around three the demons gave up, and I fell asleep. I can't remember what I dreamed, but it must have been dreadful. The next morning the sheets were soaked with sweat.

I was in the shower when I finally decided *not* to go to the Port Authority. Life was too damn short to get involved in something potentially so . . . dangerous. Besides, I had my position and reputation to protect. If the son-of-a-bitch called again, I would notify the police.

To my surprise Terry had radared bacon for breakfast. She was cautiously silent, but vaguely friendly. I really had her guessing.

"How are things going at the firm?" she asked, polishing a crystal glass.

"Oh, pretty hectic," I replied, turning the newspaper.

"Have you been trading well?" she asked, replacing the glass.

I'll let you draw the inferences from that question. It certainly wasn't my happiness she was concerned with.

"There've been a few exciting moments," I mumbled.

"But everything's going well?" she asked, leaning against the counter.

"Could be better," I replied, noticing it was bothering her.

"How bad?" she asked quickly. You see, she knew exactly how I made my living.

"We can always sell the fur coats, dear," I answered with a sigh.

"That's not exactly what the mother of two children likes to hear," she said sternly.

"Maybe they'll get football scholarships to Alabama," I replied.

She stared through the paper for several seconds, took off her apron, and left the room.

I dressed in one of my new sports jackets and left for the office about nine-thirty. The weather was cold and clear. I decided to walk a few blocks before catching a taxi.

It happened while I was in the middle of the second block. I had just told myself I could very easily stop by the Port Authority on the way to the office. But it's not like stopping for a haircut, I argued with myself. This is something that takes great thought and planning. No, my other nature insisted, you've always done important things on impulse. That's how you trade.

Without allowing my mind to dwell further on the subject I blithely hailed a cab. Be brave, I kept repeating. No guts, no glory. Nothing ventured, nothing gained. It's no worse than going to the dentist!

By the time we arrived at the Port Authority I knew why I had made the decision. First of all, I was curious. I would always wonder what the hell it had really been about. But more important, strong messages were coming from the deep, yet very large reservoirs of greed tucked neatly in the folds of my viscera. A man who could predict money supply could be wealthier than any king or emperor in the history of the world. It would be true alchemy. That's worth a little looking into.

Inside the terminal, traffic was fairly quiet. Most people who ride buses, I suppose, get to work well before 9:50. I decided to follow the instructions to the letter. I stood in the hallway, unconsciously staring at each passerby, wondering if he were my man—or woman. It crossed my mind to grab a shot of whiskey in the bar, since my stomach had begun to tremble. But I knew that early morning drinking was one of the worst signs of alcoholism, and I didn't want to add it to my already formidable list. At 10:00 I made my move.

I walked down the long hallway as a porter had directed. When I arrived at the men's room door I noticed a sign. It said "Temporarily Out of Use." My heart sank. I was about to turn away when something told me to see if the door were locked. I pushed, and it opened.

The men's room looked enormous. I stood frozen for several seconds. What to do? Dare I go in? Suppose a workman finds me? I can always say I had a very bad attack of the runs.

I walked inside and let the door swing shut. My eyes followed a long line of stalls on the right leading toward the far wall. I couldn't convince my legs to move. "Oh, what the hell!" I finally said audibly, forcing myself into motion.

I intentionally made my footsteps as loud as possible. Probably to tell myself I wasn't afraid. I pushed open the last stall and looked inside. Standard public toilet. Dirty drawings on the wall. At least there was toilet paper. I stared for a few minutes in genuine confusion. Then stepped inside.

Once inside I couldn't decide whether to remove my top coat and sports jacket or not. And then whether to take down my pants. It suddenly struck me I should. It would certainly look odd sitting on the john in the bathroom at the Port Authority at ten in the morning with a top coat and jacket on! So I hung the jacket on the hook. I placed the coat over it and let the ol' trou fall. When I finally got situated, I felt truly ridiculous.

I could hear absolutely nothing. And there was nothing to do but wait. So I waited.

Chapter 7

I'VE ALWAYS QUESTIONED the morality of greed. It seemed to me to be the very glue of civilization. After all, without an abundance of good, healthy avarice, who in the hell would ever get anything done? Henry VIII embraced the Reformation to hold on to his *things*. And look what that did for us who inherited his language? And consider most politicians today. Why would they go to the effort of operating this asylum if they weren't being well rewarded?

Now it gets out of hand occasionally. But in the long run it's the key to our genetic triumph. Mere survival would have left us in the trees. It was god-greed that sent us to the heavens.

I've always tried to keep my personal greed not only quiet, but well under control. In Christian society, it's best to do so. That's probably the biggest mistake the Russians ever made. Instead of hiding it, they outlawed it. Why, I've never truly understood. But that's why they've failed. They need to start all over. Let the greedy get rich. They'll do all the *work*.

Such wisdom was far from my thoughts as I sat on that john. First of all, it was rather chilly in the men's room. And second, in my dotage I had become susceptible to mild but easily induced cases of hemorrhoiditis. And furthermore, I was so tense I couldn't even read the rather interesting-looking graffiti.

Quite without warning, It screamed from somewhere in the toilet complex. I must have jumped a foot from sphincter reflex alone. "*It's the Godmother!*" it screamed. "*It's the Fairy Godmother!*" God, I wished I hadn't come.

"I know you're there," it moaned. "I've been watching you since you came in. And, by the way, Mr. Reed, don't try to be a bad boy and look at me. That breaks the spell. And then the fun will be over. The Godmother knows why you're here. You're here because you want to be rich and famous. You want the money supply figures. You want to trade the market with the numbers. You want . . . to . . . get . . . *rich!*"

With that She broke into grotesque laughter. I was no longer worried about hemorrhoids. There wasn't room.

"I trust you brought a pencil," She whined slowly.

I reached up to my coat and found the gold pen the staff had given me for Christmas. But I found no paper—not one goddamn scrap! I tore at the toilet roll.

"Our little favorite, M-1, will be up only two hundred million," She cooed. "That's a surprise to most of my little children. But the little rascal M-2 will be flat. Oooooh, that should be a little giggle."

I struggled to make legible impressions on the toilet paper. I vowed never to gripe about the city of New York again. The stuff was as hard as cardboard.

"Our little M-3 is a bad girl this week," She continued.

"She's up only two hundred and fifty million. Isn't that sassy?"

I was so intent on writing the figures I completely forgot where I was or with whom I was talking. In fact, a strange sense of security replaced my abject paranoia. The Godmother was giving me the figures. That was all that counted.

"I'm going to leave now, Mr. Reed," She intoned. "You should stay on the pottie for at least five minutes before leaving. You'll hear from me this weekend. Godmother loves you. Be a *good boy.*"

I heard nothing from that point on. And I didn't move for five minutes.

I left the bathroom feeling much like the child who'd been told by the doctor he needed no shots. I stepped light on my feet and was moved to whistle. I raced toward the taxi stand to head for the office.

When I arrived, I went to my cubicle and shut the door. I ordered a cup of coffee and quickly checked the markets. The boys were expecting *much* higher money supply figures the next day because of the big drop the previous week. All bonds were under pressure. The coffee arrived, and I sat back to organize my strategy.

There was a point when I had decided to let the lads in on my little adventure with the Godmother. It would make a great story if She were right for two straight weeks. But then I realized I couldn't *possibly* tell them if She were right for two straight weeks. That alone would kick off a tremendous investigation by somebody. And that would mean an end to the fun. And to the profit.

After sipping the coffee for five minutes, I decided to take a flier. I was going to buy heavily into the declining market. It would really make me look bad if She was wrong. And, hell, I knew in my heart-of-hearts there was no way for Her to be right. But it was a once in a lifetime shot, and why not? It wasn't my money.

The rest of the day I quietly began buying bonds—all coupons and all maturities. I didn't want to make a big splash, just in case I was wrong. By the end of the day I had bought over a hundred and fifty million at prices significantly lower. By three o'clock I was so excited I thought about really loading up. But I remembered we had still another day. I would wait to see how the market opened the following morning.

I left the office about five. I started to drop by Janet's office, but I remembered she always got her hair done Wednesday afternoons. Instead I went straight home, almost giving Terry a heart attack when I walked in at five-thirty. I asked if she would join me in a libation, and her face lighted up for the first time in two years. We even had a nice conversation. She had had a pleasant luncheon with the girls before attending the St. Sebastian's annual fashion show. She then went shopping and found the most marvelous shoes at Bergdorf's—of all places! I even asked to see the shoes and marveled at their beauty. For $125 they looked pretty nice.

We then discussed the boys' grades—the younger one

had discovered girls that year—and went over the plans for the March trip to Lost Tree. She wanted me to get a new summer tuxedo. I was well into the third martini at this stage and felt I had done quite enough good-willing. So midsentence I reached over and flipped on the Happy News network to see what wasn't really happening that day in Israel. She got the message and ran off to take something from the freezer. I finished the martini and made another one.

Dinner was extremely dull, which made me regretful I had been so nice over drinks. Besides, I couldn't get Her off my mind. I was finding it truly exciting. It was like playing fantasy as a child. Something for nothing. Tooth fairy. Santa Claus.

I lay in bed for several hours, periodically reading the book between long, clear cogitations over the markets. There was nothing concrete I could do until I knew whether She knew what She was doing. I didn't even want to think about what would happen if the dream came true. About eleven, I thought about sneaking over to Terry's room and sweet-talking a piece of ass. But her sex drive had turned to cooked celery since the hysterectomy. Besides, there was Janet. And I had something even more exciting to think about than sex. And someone far more exciting than a beautiful woman.

I had to spend the entire following morning in an executive committee meeting. That's where all the top management—they're the guys in the really tight pinstripes—chew pipes and practice affectations that are supposed to make them sound as if they came from Old Banking Families in England. After hearing the hundredth cliché—"Bite the bullet"; "The paper was so bogus you needed a mirror to read it"; "Things must go down before they go up"—I let my mind wander back to the magic hour of four o'clock. If She were wrong, I could forget about the whole mess and go back to normal. If She were right—well, don't even think about it. It's impossible!

We all went to lunch, and I purred in the chairman's ear that successful bond trading was like a winning squash game. I drank very little at those affairs. Why tempt fate? It was insufferably dull.

I closed the door to the office to watch the electronic screen. I wasn't sure how I would react when the figures were flashed. I had always been rather aloof about money supply. I'd hate for the boys to see me drool in my afternoon tea.

The minutes before four seemed like eons. I wished I had a radio to hear classical music. Finally, the digital clock on the desk began ticking the final minute. I began pounding on the top of the desk.

And then it began trickling across the screen:

THE MONEY SUPPLY FIGURES AS REPORTED BY THE
FEDERAL RESERVE SYSTEM FOR THE WEEK ENDING FEB. 4:
M-1 INCREASED A SCANT $200 MILLION DOLLARS. M-2
REMAINED UNCHANGED . . .

Chapter 8

I'VE NEVER BEEN a big jogger. The Park was too dangerous—even in daytime—and one small pile of dog dung could completely destroy an elbow. But that was all I could decide to do. My entire being was in turmoil, and I figured involving the entire person in an activity was the only solution.

I ran in the Park—despite the danger. Every time the pain became a problem, I would remind myself there was no alternative. I got more exercise in that hour than in the previous six months. You see, the markets rallied on the money figures. They rallied a half a point in the first twenty minutes. That means the firm made over seven hundred and fifty thousand dollars on the little hundred and fifty million I had bought Wednesday. That's not going to make or break me or the firm, but it could have been ten times that amount—or a hundred. Knowing the figures can make the desert bloom. It's like playing God.

And it was a whole new ballgame with the Godmother. If She could predict the figures two straight weeks, She was obviously wired into the truth. I had to believe that no such person existed, yet I had to deal with the facts. Two straight weeks. Right on the money. What the hell to do now?

I'm not an unreasonably selfish person. The firm had

been very nice to me. I would have loved to return the favor by making it the banker to the world. But there would have been no way, week after week, to be right on money supply without being detected. It's too serious even to discuss. That means there was only one way to exploit the information properly, and that was through personal gain. But dare I? How? Was it still possibly a freakish coincidence?

The first and overwhelming question was the possible criminal liability. Even if it were possible—and it wasn't—for someone with money supply figures at the Federal Reserve to contact me, would it be illegal for me to benefit from them? Or, if the Fairy Godmother were for real—or for *un*real, if you see what I mean—would that too be illegal? After all, the only free lunch is social security. I knew I would have to answer those questions. But where?

That evening I was sitting at a horse show at the Garden. You guessed it. Terry's cousin was Master of the Hunt in Charlottesville and was showing her jumper for top honors. I never minded the horse shows, though, since most of the riders were seventeen-year-old girls with well-developed thigh and butt muscles.

Just as some lass was taking the last jump, I spied Reuben Kollar. He was a Midwesterner who had come to Gotham to claim fame and fortune in the legal ring. I had always liked him because he was a gentle old drunk. We used to play bridge at the Racquet. He was excellent until the sixth or seventh bourbon.

I waited till Matilda's Rover knocked over the last rail

and then stood up. He was only a few rows away and looked thoroughly slippered. I waltzed across a barrier and slid into the seat next to him like a long lost fraternity brother selling life insurance.

"Hey, Reuben?" I said, extending the hand. "How's the old finesse?"

Reuben expressed mock surprise and extended his dealer's hand. "Could complain, but won't," he replied. "What you up to?"

We exchanged the normal pleasantries concerning wives, kids, dogs, et cetera, and turned our eyes toward the latest young entrant. Sadly, the two of us sat engrossed for several minutes as the lithesome thing squeezed her horse's behind over several jumps before running him through a hazard. I felt I knew what she was experiencing.

I then took ten dollars out of my pocket and gave it to him. "This is for professional consultation," I began. "It may get more serious."

I watched Reuben pocket the ten dollars, so felt compelled to say something. Unfortunately I didn't know where to begin. And surely he didn't want to give advice at a horse show to some potential Spiro Agnew. How could I phrase the questions? What were the questions?

"Well, what is it, Stud?" he mumbled through his cigar. "Knocked up the secretary?"

"No, no," I replied, smiling broadly to let him know *that* really wasn't the case. "No, it involves . . . it involves a . . . pure question of law."

"Fire, Professor," he mumbled again. "I've always been fascinated with purity."

"If . . . if a government employee . . . obtained—"

"You mean 'stole,' " he interrupted laconically.

"Well . . . not *stole*, but—"

"Don't do it," he mumbled before taking a big puff and flicking the ashes. "Our types don't hold up too well in the Big House."

"What . . . what . . . responsibility—"

"Oh, a moral duty as a citizen, I suppose," he groaned, shifting one weighty leg over the other. "But it's one most *citizens* find easy to overlook. To know is to forgive, et cetera. Just stay clear and forget it—if you can."

"Oh, I *can*," I assured him. "Most certainly!"

"Here's your change," he murmured, pulling eight dollars from a large roll. "The fee will buy a nice Havana. That is, if I want to overlook the moral responsibility I have as a citizen not to buy contraband."

I felt like a school kid who had been chastised and then forgiven by the principal. I couldn't get an answer from him without spilling all the beans—or without sounding like a lunatic. Fairy Godmother? I could see the expression on Reuben's face.

I continued sitting next to the silent hulk, not knowing what to do next. He was a damned good lawyer. He could tell even from the question—and the hesitancy—there was something wrong. And, of course, I knew it was wrong. The figures didn't mean anything financially to the government, but they were certainly important to the rest of the world. Surely it's a crime to . . . steal them—if that's what it was. I would have to operate on that assumption. I was into something illegal. I've never done anything illegal in my life. Nothing truly important, at least. I couldn't do it. I didn't have the stomach.

Another sleepless night, my thoughts going from one extreme to another. At one point I was a glamorous international spy. The next minute I experienced horrible thoughts of public shame, bankruptcy, terror, getting raped or knifed in a cold, gray, concrete prison cell. No friends. No family. Alone. Forgotten.

To say I was depressed the next morning is a misstatement. I was suicidal. My whole life was coming to an end. I barely spoke at the office, even though my little seven-hundred-fifty-thousand-dollar triumph was privately being attributed to my absolute clairoyance. If the Fairy Godmother was a federal employee, and anything *but* a real, true-to-life, honest-to-God Fairy Godmother—and I mean one with *wings*—I was out. I wasn't going to do it. I didn't have the stomach.

By four I was desperate. I called a fellow named Phillip Van Nice, who used to work at the Fed. I was rather blunt. I had to have an answer. I asked if it were possible to know the figures. His reply was a laugh. Even the President couldn't get them. And then I asked if it was criminal for an employee to pass them out. The answer was a grunt. "I guess so. The question never came up. After all, it would be too easy to detect."

"What do you mean?"

"You couldn't be right every week without being caught," he answered. "But why the questions? What's going on? This is really silly."

I explained I was giving a lecture at Rutgers Banking School in the spring and needed some jokes. He understood.

There was only one solution. I took to drink. I went even further. I called Janet and told her it was imperative we spend the weekend together on the Island. She protested until I told her it was a question of life and death. I told Terry I was driving to see the boat. I wanted to know that it was still there. The boat. The last certainty in my surging sea.

Somehow it all worked, and I found myself safely en-sconced in an empty, little motel near the Hamptons. We drifted off to a small seaside restaurant several miles away. There was a fire which glistened against the swirling, sea-angry snow. During the second Scotch and soda, she asked, "What the hell's the matter?"

I felt like crying. No one had asked the question. No one seemed to give a damn. They all thought the guru was impervious to doubts. To fear. I raised my face to the window, feeling myself partner to the storm-tossed flakes racing through the shadowless night. I began a reply, but my voice failed.

"Tell me, baby," she asked softly, her eyes moistening. "I'm not going to hurt."

"It's . . . it's—"

"It must really hurt," she whispered, moving her hand toward mind. "Maybe I can help."

"It's so hard to explain," I replied, my head falling. "Without sounding . . . crazy."

"Oh, listen," she said, squeezing my hand. "We know each other too well for that."

"Well, suppose there was another side to me?" I asked. "Suppose I had fears . . . and doubts?"

"Oh, Bobby," she moaned. "We all have those. The bigger we are, the worse we hurt."

"Well, what would you think—"

"Telephone for Mr. Reed!" the waiter chirped. "Are you Mr. Reed?"

I nodded, my mouth agape. Yes, I am Mr. Reed. Husband of Mrs. Reed. The ballgame's over.

Chapter 9

THE PLOT WAS THICKENING, but unfortunately I was in the middle of it. It wasn't my wife's lawyer. It was She.

And She wasn't nice at all. An austere, even sinister, tone was in Her voice. Thoughts of the kidnapping returned. There was no joking about the figures either, no—excuse the expression—"motherliness." She was all business. I was to meet her at the National Botanical Gardens in Washington the following Tuesday at two o'clock. I was to sit on a bench next to the giant date palm—*Phoenix dactylifera*, she informed me—for exactly five minutes. Then I was to leave the building through the side entrance. I was then to proceed around the building to the entrance nearest the Capitol and reenter through the azaleas. *And*, before making the tour, I was to leave an envelope containing five thousand dollars placed inside a copy of *Winnie the Pooh*.

Well, at least I knew the Godmother was human. That is, until She went berserk and began screeching because I had called Phillip Van Nice. I almost wet my pants. How in the hell did She know that? For God's sake, Phillip couldn't have called Her! Whom was I dealing with? What didn't She know? The anxiety returned. And, you guessed it, I couldn't get an erection.

What preoccupied me the next several days was the fact I hadn't asked if She were going to give me the new figures. Maybe it was a shell game. But that didn't make sense. If She had the information, She wouldn't try to con five grand from some lonesome bond trader. But that meant there was now money involved. Bribery. Prison! Oh, God, I wished it hadn't happened. Confusion. Total confusion.

I must have started to dial Reuben ten times, but each time I hung up the telephone. The only advice he could give would be a resounding no. Besides, he wouldn't understand. There was no way for someone to get that information. I had actually begun to wonder whether the Godmother were supernatural.

And the money. The five thousand. That's a lot of money! Certainly enough to send you to Atlanta for five years. Why me? Why this agony?

Another interesting development had occurred. Janet became convinced I had cancer of the brain. She even told me her suspicions. Terry, on the other hand, confessed she thought I had been drinking too much. "For twenty years, in fact," she finally blurted out. Kind hearts, really.

Things at the office were calm. My abnormalities were quietly attributed to a growing synthesis of the personality with the higher self. It's what Beethoven and Einstein apparently experienced upon approaching their greatest moments.

Well, before I tell you, I must tell you *why*. And then how. As I've said, I'm not a greedy man. At least no greedier than your average liberal, urban, upper middle-class Democrat—which I'm not. But, you see, I recently turned forty. I was still in good shape, but the old telltale signs were there. I had a wretched marriage and a clandestine liaison which was promising—at best. I was stuck in a very standard job, performing a very insignificant function—if you stop and think about it. I really didn't like where I lived. I couldn't relate to my children, although I loved them. I had no truly close friends—male or female. I didn't want some day to be sixty-two—with no alternatives. I didn't want the retirement house in Connecticut. The tiny two-sailer. The four weeks every February in Tucson. Possibly, just possibly, She was offering me something different. Something I had never done. Excitement, you might call it. Perhaps fantasy.

The morality of the situation was the toughest question. We all steal paperclips occasionally, but this certainly had larger overtones. At first I felt it was like embezzling from the firm. But, after all, the information was being given to *me*, not the firm. And I would have to use my own capital to take advantage of it, not someone else's. And I guess the information gave me a tremendous advantage versus the other traders, but, hell, brains do the same thing. And I hadn't actually solicited the numbers. For that matter, I was probably an idiot for betting a fortune on the ravings of some psychopath. As far as I was concerned, it was the same as getting them from a newspaper. And better me than some foreigner. Imagine if they fell into the hands of a Soviet spy?

On Monday afternoon I went to the bank and withdrew the five thousand dollars. I had heard that banks must report large cash withdrawals. Sounds like Russia, but it's apparently true. I explained I was buying my wife a fur coat for her birthday. The teller wasn't much interested. I always bought with cash, I explained. You get better deals that way. Still no response. You ought to try it, I continued. The next time you buy a five-thousand-dollar coat.

Try taking five thousand in cash home some night without telling your wife. I felt like a teenager hiding *Playboy* from his mother. She knew something was wrong when I didn't take my coat off in the hall. And I was nervous all evening that she'd go back to the bedroom and search it. My God, if she had found that money! I can't even imagine the accusations. Come to think of it, I wouldn't have blamed her. Oh, it's to give to the Fairy Godmother, dear!

For some reason I had a rather restful night, although the anxiety returned during breakfast. I didn't tell her I was leaving town, but I did mention something about meetings all day.

It had been years since I had been on a real train. And, frankly, I was rather impressed. Being in the securities business, I was always somewhat amused by the government's destruction of our railroad system, and naturally I expected the worst. They were neat, somewhat clean. Very fast. And, surprisingly, only three times as expensive as they used to be.

I brought lots to read, and settled back for the two hours

to our nation's capital. I had forgotten how beautiful were parts of New Jersey and Delaware. In my middle age I had become something of a conservationist, you see. If we're going to give all that money away, it might as well be to save the countryside.

Sights of water and forests brought back memories of childhood. Don't let me mislead you, I was city born and bred. But one doesn't grow up in Michigan without experiencing a whole lot of outdoors. At least not back in the forties and fifties. Especially if you were a Boy Scout. How far I had come. How much I had changed. I felt sad, almost as if it were Christmas Eve. I thought of my children. My father. I wondered what they would think of me if they knew my mission. They wouldn't believe me.

The train pulled into the old Union Station. Remembrances of a childhood trip raced through my mind. Also John Kennedy dead. Eisenhower giving the country to the rich. Truman bidding a sad farewell. It was noon. I needed something to eat before the rendezvous. I asked the porter for a good restaurant, and he suggested the Martha Washington. I thought it was a joke, but it wasn't. It was just a few blocks away, directly across from the Senate Office Building. I caught a cab, settled into a nice booth, and ordered a martini. I might as well have been in New York.

I ordered calf's liver with bacon. I felt I needed iron. It came with a salad and was delicious, especially with a glass of French burgundy. The trip wasn't a total loss. As I ate I watched the comings and goings of what must have been congressmen and lobbyists. At least the Godmother and I had the good taste to try to cover up our chicanery. These guys even write it off their income taxes.

At fifteen till two I stepped out onto the snow-covered sidewalk and hailed a cab. I told the driver I wanted to go to the National Botanical Gardens. He said he'd never heard of it. In fact, he had been driving a cab for thirteen years, and he would bet the fare it didn't exist. Trusting in the Old Lady, I told him the bet was on. He studied his little book for several seconds, then let out with a low "Motherfuck. Will ya look at dat?"

He mumbled as he drove the several blocks it took to get there. When we arrived at the front of the old *beaux arts* structure, he did nothing but shake his head and stare. I thanked him very much and hopped out. I should have told him my Fairy Godmother had sent me there, but I was afraid that would have provoked a fistfight.

I strode into the main entrance and immediately found myself surrounded by thousands of azalea plants. The warm, sticky atmosphere and lush, vivid colors left me momentarily disoriented. I asked a workman the location of the giant date palm, and he pointed me toward a path through another door. The next room was planted as a jungle, and I had to remove my coat. It occurred to me that She was probably there somewhere watching me. I felt a chill despite the heat. I finally spotted the tree and the bench. I sat down and immediately realized my greatest error. I had forgotten the damn *Winnie the Pooh*!

I felt like such an idiot. How could I have forgotten to buy it? It was too late to go get one. It was two minutes till two, and that would certainly queer the rendezvous. I could have killed myself. I had come all that way, and I was going to blow it!

There was only one thing to do. In case She was watching me, I stuck the envelope with the money inside my overcoat pocket and left it on the bench. I hoped She would put two and two together. I began walking nervously toward the side entrance. As I neared it, a group of rough-looking Latino kids passed by, headed toward the giant date palm. I paused to turn back, but knew the Godmother would never forgive me for such an indiscretion. I gulped hard and left the building. It was very cold without an overcoat, and walking through the snow with street shoes was painful. I finally decided to run. As I rounded the corner nearest the Capitol, I slipped and fell on my ass. I cursed, knowing those damned kids were stealing the five thousand and that I was the biggest fool in financial history. Panting, I reached the entrance and rushed inside. The warm air hit me like a hard wave, and I was seized with a sneezing spell. I ran through the azaleas, trying to find the bench. Each way I took seemed to lead toward some other part of the gardens. I became disoriented and felt like crying out to Her to help me find my way. Suddenly, through the foliage, I spied the bench. I couldn't determine which path to take, so I stepped over the barrier and waded through the vines and soggy earth.

"Hey, get out of there!" a voice shouted. I reached the bench and saw the coat in a different position from that in which I had left it. My heart pounded, as I grabbed it. I pounded the pocket to see if the envelope was there. It was gone.

"Don't you have no respect for government property," the angry voice demanded. "This is a national treasure. You think you can just climb anywhere you want?"

Oblivious to the sound, I stood silently holding the coat. Believe it or not, I was crying—inside. I had screwed up her instructions. I had lost the five thousand, simply because I was careless. And now the whole deal was probably off.

I turned to the gardener, a black man, and said, "I'm terribly sorry, but I got lost. I'll be glad to pay for any damage."

Perhaps it was the tremor in my voice which made him calm down. He mumbled something and turned to leave. I slowly pulled on the overcoat and looked around for the exit. I reached in my pocket for a glove and pulled out a piece of paper. There, in an elaborate, wispy script was written "M-1 down 2.1B; M-2 down 2.6B; M-3 down 3.1B. Much love, F.G."

Chapter 10

I WAS EXHAUSTED when I reached New York. And I was also drunk. The new trains had very nice bar service. I had had a lot of time to think during the trip, and drink was the only legitimate out. I went over each question of the past days. And nothing was any clearer. I was, however, able to come to one conclusion. I was going to do it. Despite the risks—the insanity—of the whole matter, I was going to follow the trail further. There seemed to be no alternative. What else was there to live for, goddammit? What else, at this age, would come my way later? But it was becoming, I had to admit it, fun. Exciting.

And—believe this too, if you wish—I was beginning to like Her. I had no idea who or what She was, but I liked Her style. And, yes, I had confidence in Her. I felt She would take care of me. Like a real—sorry, friend—Fairy Godmother.

Terry wasn't that kind when I stumbled in the door. She too had had time to think and apparently had decided to revert to the art of the diatribe. I desperately needed something to eat, so spastically ransacked the refrigerator while listening to her noise. I shoved a sandwich on a large plate and walked to my room. She followed me, so I shut the door and locked it. I wolfed down the sandwich and hurried to bed. Perhaps—no, certainly—I kept telling myself, there was somewhere ahead a better deal than this. I had to get to sleep. I had a big day ahead.

I rode to the office the following morning in a cheerful mood. It was an almost childlike enthusiasm, one which I hadn't experienced since my early twenties, and it felt good. All eyes followed me as I wound through the myriad desks toward the cubicle. I knew what they wanted—like caged animals at the feeding time. It was the food. The bread of life. They wanted the money figures. Straight from the guru's hand.

My problem, unfortunately, was to keep it from them. Three correct predictions in a row would have aroused the suspicions of a rock. I shut the door and ordered coffee. I had to act fairly quickly, and I had to be careful. One screwup, and it might be over.

The coffee came, and I smiled as if I were still savoring the sensations of a pleasant weekend. As soon as the door shut, I reached for the telephone and called old Worthington Hess, a classmate at Wharton.

Worthington—he preferred that to "Worth"—was from a Wilmington family of impeccable credentials, if dwindling resources. He was sent to the grad school at some sacrifice in the hopes he might help shore up the otherwise dubious condition of the trusts. Unfortunately, the family didn't quite realize that Worth himself made the present trustee look like Lord Keynes. He was—to put it kindly—one of the densest people of this century.

Our relationship truly melded during school when I helped him arrange an abortion for an Italian girl he was seeing. I think he could have survived the raised eyebrows in Delaware, but the poor girl kept saying, "My God, the brothers! They'll kill you! If they find out I'm not a virgin, they'll kill you!"

Good ol' Hess valiantly offered to marry her, but he wasn't a Catholic. I guess in Salerno it's better to kill a baby than share the house with an Anglican.

Well, I had a friend who was an intern at Philadelphia General, and he arranged for an examination with a buddy in gynecology. The buddy was convinced the mother would hemorrhage to death if she were forced to deliver, so at four in the morning one awful winter's Sunday, they gave her the old goose. The girl disappeared—somewhat to Worthington's chagrin—and I had a devotee for life.

But that's not all. Four or five years later—after he had hitched up with one of the Bigs from Wilmington—he did it again. Only this time it was a Jewish girl. Her brothers weren't going to kill him. They were going to bankrupt him!

We pulled the same number. The gynecologist buddy was in practice in Short Hills, New Jersey. We arranged an examination which discovered she had a heart murmur. Four in the morning—Bingo!—out it splashed. Along with twenty thousand dollars for "recuperation."

Needless to say, Worthington felt an even closer loyalty toward me. And, fortunately, he happened to be working in New York as an officer in a large commodity firm. His voice was enthusiastic when I called him. He was anxious to repay the debts.

We chatted about wives, children, friends, and old times. We then wondered why we hadn't seen much of each other the past several years. They rarely got into the city, you see. I then asked what he knew about the bond futures at the Chicago Board of Trade. He was most positive and suggested I open an account. I informed him that was against the firm's rules, but that I would like to hear the details. He caught on—Worthington wasn't *that* dumb—and suggested I trade through his account. I told him that would be unfair because it might complicate his income taxes. Actually I was afraid the fool might go nuts and take some of the money.

Worthington hadn't forgotten, however, my earlier munificence and offered to be of any help he could. I said I wanted to open an account in a totally fictitious name. He laughed nervously and informed me that was out of the question. I returned the laugh and informed him I would call his wife on the WATS line if it weren't arranged. He asked for the spelling of the fictitious name.

The social-security number was the bugaboo. I knew the Feds never checked it against trading accounts but, still, twenty years from now they might. Russia again. I figured the odds were a hundred to one it would make any difference, so I made one up. The rest of it was child's play. I gave him the name of Herman Gottmutter. He protested, but all I had to do was mention the name of my favorite Italian *ristorante*.

After the traumatics both of us calmed down, and he asked what I wanted to do with the account. I told him I wanted to trade the bond futures at the Board of Trade. He sighed the sigh of the reprieved—there were scandals in the grains—and informed me there would be a twelve-hundred-dollar margin deposit for each contract. I informed him I meant to trade at least a hundred contracts—ten million dollars' worth of futures—and he gasped. Meekly he informed me that that would be one hundred and twenty thousand dollars up front. I hummed a few notes from "Have Nagila."

We spent a few minutes arguing over the risks of the position and all the audit problems before I cleared my throat. I then informed him I was in a position to write to Wharton to reveal the fact I had written his senior project. It was rough, but that's how one had to deal with Worthington. He was too good—or too stupid—to take care of himself. Much less me.

The rest of the conversation was spent dealing with the arrangements for the execution of the trades. I would call him the following day to tell him what I wanted to do. He was to put me on the three-way line with the phone man on the floor of the Board of Trade. He was to say nothing to anyone. Because if my firm found out, I would lose my job. That was a nice touch, I thought.

I spent the rest of the day performing perfunctory duties. I called my brethren at the opposition and found out money was called unchanged. Therefore, I suggested to the firm that we not speculate. That wasn't bad advice with the government we had. One could never guess what those fools might do within a twenty-four-hour period.

I walked all the way home from the office. The weather had warmed, and a rain the night before had cleared most of the snow and dog dung away. The air was clear, and the traffic sparse. Except for the fear of mugging, it was a delightful hour in the city. I wasn't remotely tired when I reached the neighborhood, so I turned and walked toward a local tavern. There was no one I recognized at the bar, so I sat for two Scotches observing how the ordinary lead their lives. It was pretty discouraging. One old gal next to me—in a five-figure mink coat—insisted on berating her companion about their doorman. The cop on my right insisted on telling the barman each detail of the Bears game against San Francisco. The New York cop was actually a Bears fan! I grew bored and left, placing a nice tip on the bar. I stumbled a few times as I made my way toward the apartment. When I opened the door, I noticed everything was dark. I was disturbed at first. After all, I was a couple hours late. But to hell with her, I told myself. If she's not here, to *hell* with her. I stumbled toward the bed, knowing I should at least eat something. I managed to remove part of the clothing. I was tired. I had a lot to do the following day. She should be with me. She should be helping me. But with Terry it's all take, take, take. Then I thought of Her. Her generosity. The things to come. The beauty of the morning. The excitement of the day. The feeling of well-being. And I went to sleep.

Chapter 11

THE EXPERIENCE HAD actually excited me sexually. That befuddled me until I remembered the swimming meets back in high school. Hiding it in those little swim trunks made my present subterfuge seem like child's play. It was easily remedied, however. I called Janet and arranged a date for the evening. She was relieved to hear from me, especially when I innocently suggested we go to dinner at a new restaurant mentioned in the *Times*. None of the wife's friends would be caught dead eating in a place written up in the *Times*.

Oh, Terry. It seems she had left a note in the hallway explaining she was working late on a spring charity ball. I mumbled loudly to myself about getting my eyes checked and left as quickly for the office as I could.

I had sat tensely at my desk knowing that the moment of truth had arrived. I was about to strike out for personal gain. I was also about to seal the bond with a crook, even though I still couldn't believe She was real. I hate to repeat this, but it's truly impossible. I could even hear the tick of the digital clock on my desk. I was scared, but I was drinking deeply from the cup of life. I was exhilarated. I could feel my whole body.

I picked up the telephone and called Worthington. I had to wait while they found him. Once he came on the line he fumbled with the conference call. I was irritated, but could understand his nervousness.

We finally reached the floor broker who was panting from the opening activities. The market was trading off—no one knew why—the local traders were pushing it—there was some support from orders, but not enough—if you want to sell it, do it now. I shouted—despite my agreement with Worthington not to speak on the telephone—to buy a hundred contracts at the present levels. We waited anxiously, hearing nothing but cacophony in the background. My face was hot, and I could feel my heart beat. I was, in effect, buying ten million dollars' worth of securities. If the market broke—if She were *wrong!*—I could lose a fortune. Fifty, even a hundred thousand dollars. I had never traded my own money before. I suddenly wanted out. I didn't have the stomach for it.

Just at that moment the broker returned to the telephone to announce breathlessly he had bought fifty-five contracts at sixteen thirty-seconds and the balance at fifteen. It was a good execution. Worthington thanked him and disconnected with the trading floor. I was so stunned I found nothing to say. He too was speechless. "That's a lot of stuff," he finally whispered. "Sure is," I replied. "You know what you're doing?" he asked. "Sure do," I answered confidently. "Call you later."

I spent the rest of the morning in the commodities section of the firm watching the quotations. I explained I was getting ready to do a cash-market arbitrage for the firm against the futures. The commodity idiots got excited and began asking me all sorts of elementary questions. It was driving me nuts, but I couldn't leave. I had a fortune riding on the position.

The futures market continued to slip most of the morning, as did the cash markets. By noon it was seven thirty-seconds lower—every thirty-second costing me roughly three thousand dollars. I got so nervous I finally went back to the office and called Worthington again. He was even more jittery. He knew I could probably handle a twenty-thousand-dollar loss, but he was worried I had lost my mind. I asked him to get the floor broker on the telephone. The broker said the market was simply drifting. There just weren't many buyers.

I hung up the telephone and thought for several seconds. If the Godmother was correct, the market would rally like mad. If I was unwilling to buy more at this stage, I should never have bought the first hundred. I called Worthington again and told him to get the broker. I ordered the broker to buy another hundred contracts. I could hear Worthington wretching into his wastebasket. Poor bastard. He could see his whole career going down the drain, no doubt.

I left the office immediately and walked toward the Battery. A fog had descended upon the lower end of Manhattan, reducing the older parts of the area to the village it once was. Oddly there was very little traffic. Even the sounds of the city were muted. I sat on a bench overlooking the river and savored my sensations. Normally when I traded for the firm I experienced a vague depression until everything was resolved. I once decided that that was because the anxiety was a constant reminder that I was "hired help." That I was a faceless cog in the firm's money machine. But that afternoon I felt somehow released. Oh, surely, there was some anxiety. But it was the tremendous sense of freedom that made me want to stand and stretch. Possibly, just possibly, I was on my way. I could be truly my own man. I could be free.

Well, you can guess the rest. Godmother came in right on the money, and the market rallied with an explosion. I knew that on the morrow the futures market would rise sixteen to twenty thirty-seconds. That would mean a profit of over a hundred thousand dollars. I had never felt so good in my entire life. I just sat in my chair with a big grin and shook my head.

Worthington called, his voice sounding like that of a politician found innocent of a bribery charge. "Boy, was that lucky!" he shouted. That's not the way we suggest a customer trade, but it sure worked!" I told him to liquidate half the position on the next morning's open and to call me when it was done. I hung up without chatting. I didn't want to waste those wonderful moments listening to his inane compliments.

The dinner with Janet was exquisite. For the first time ever, I felt I knew her really well. She was no longer just an attractive lay. And I didn't need to be cute or try to act young. In fact, most of the evening I said very little. I simply sat next to her, touching her with my shoulder. Twice she asked why I was so quiet, and I simply grinned.

Later I told her it was because I was so happy. I even took her hand and stroked it on top of the table, a practice I find particularly distasteful in older lechers.

"You act like the cat who ate the canary," she purred, licking the chocolate mousse.

"Yeah, I feel pretty good," I replied, feeling as if I owed a response.

"That's what I really like about you," she said, scraping the sides of the dish. "You're not afraid to show your emotions. Most men are, you know. They think it makes them look small or something."

I was a little taken back with the compliment, so took a sip of the cognac.

"Well, that makes you something special too," I finally said. "Most women want the man to be . . . impervious to . . . doubt . . ."

"Yeah, but a smart woman knows that's impossible," she winked, touching my hand. "Who wants some clod who couldn't feel fear? It's frightening even to fall in love."

Later we went to her apartment where I had the strangest experience. I had taken off my clothes and climbed into bed while she was in the bathroom. The drapes to her bedroom were closed, and—with the lights out—I wanted them opened. As I pulled the drapes back I was surprised by the beautiful view of the city, and especially the Park. I stood there naked, absorbed by the peacefulness of the sparkling visage and by the strange sensations inside me. I felt new. And ageless. And I felt somehow cleansed of years of accumulated fears and habits. I felt I was sensing my true self for the first time, instead of the self-image half built on the demands and opinions of others.

She emerged from the bathroom and slipped into the bed. She asked what I was doing, but I didn't feel she was demanding a reply. I remained standing there a long time, feeling as if I were flying above the buildings below and beyond. And enjoying those feelings more than the sexual feast I knew awaited me.

She said nothing, but simply continued to watch me. I appreciated that. She was accepting me too. Naked. Silent. Eventually I turned and went to her.

The sum came to a hundred and fourteen thousand and some odd dollars. Normally I looked at the "odd dollars," but not with a hit like that. It was a whole new world for me now. I wasn't going to worry about the pennies.

It was going to a great deal more trouble than I had anticipated, however. The first problem was what to do about Worthington. That idiot would very quickly get aroused if I started making a couple hundred grand a month on Fridays only. And there was just enough thief in him to try to get in on the act.

The second problem struck even closer to home. What the hell was I going to do about the income taxes? I didn't mind *paying* the taxes—eventually I could treat it all as long-term capital gain. And the last thing in the world I wanted to do was go to jail for evasion. But a routine audit might create suspicion in a government official. It would take some time and thinking.

I drove out to the harbor on the Island for the weekend to work on my boat. I asked Terry several times if she would come, knowing she wouldn't. It was too inclement to get a suntan, and all the shops were closed. What else does one go to the sea for? I was delighted, of course, because—knowing she would decline—I had arranged for Janet to come help me.

The work was easy—I always let the marina do the tough stuff—and gave me perfect opportunity to pull everything together. The smell of the water, the taste of steamed clams and white wine, and the feel of Janet's legs and thighs provided two most memorable days. And I also finished the last of the bothersome maritime chores before spring.

On Monday I called Worthington and withdrew seventy-five thousand. He said a clerk would bring the check by the office before noon. As soon as the check arrived, I put on my coat and walked down Wall Street to the offices of a large commodity firm that had no interests in the bond markets. I met a very nice older man and introduced myself with my real name. I opened an account with a personal check for seventy-five thousand. I told him I was retired and worked out of my home. I then told him I had been playing the commodities for about ten years and had grown tired of the grains. I had been studying the bond futures and wanted to try some. He wasn't too familiar with bond futures, but promised to study up over the next couple of days—so he could make recommendations. I almost gagged.

I gave him a fictitious social-security number. I figured

if the Russians in Washington ever caught me, the social-security number would be the smallest of offenses.

I decided to wait to solve the income tax problem. One swallow doesn't make a summer. After all, Godmother might vanish as quickly as She arrived.

Chapter 12

AND VANISH SHE DID. I really hadn't expected to hear from Her over the weekend, but I was disturbed when I hadn't received a message by Tuesday. The new commodity broker had called me on Monday evening at home—as instructed—and had given me some incredibly stupid recommendation. I told him I would think about it and call him, probably on Wednesday. Everything was set. All She had to do was let me know where to pick up the figures.

Still nothing all day Wednesday. I left a bit early and dropped by Cartier's to pick up a little celebration for the girls. I bought Terry a fifteen-hundred-dollar brooch. That would keep her busy for a while. And I bought Janet a heavy silver necklace from Sweden. I found myself putting much more thought into Janet's gift, for some reason. Perhaps because it would look better on her firm, young bosom. When it came time to pay, it suddenly hit me. She wasn't *going* to call. It was already too late. I certainly couldn't get to Washington in time. It was probably all over.

By the time I got home I was depressed. Even the glimmer of treasure in Terry's eyes failed to lift my spirits. I hadn't had much to drink for the week, so fell into the gin bottle. Terry even helped me get undressed around ten.

Thursday I was particularly down. The boys still hadn't

forgotten my previous triumphs and continued to press me for a prediction. The Street was calling it "unchanged," so I followed suit. Worthington called about noon pestering me for an order. I lectured him that truly successful speculators get rich—and stay rich—through patience and that I was waiting until I felt the time was right. I knew why he was so anxious. He wanted to tail me—put on a few for himself. Whether it was out of cruelty or good sense, I told him to buy me ten contracts at the market. Whatever the money supply figures were, the market was due for a little downward correction. If it were unchanged, it would surely sell off five to ten points. The couple of thousand dollars' loss would be a small price to pay, to get Worthington off my back.

Everybody lingered around the Telerate screen until three, to see what the figures would be, and sure enough they were unchanged. I suppressed a giggle as I watched the prices slide five, then six, thirty-seconds.

It was colder, but I decided to walk home. I was scheduled to see Janet at eight—"There's a big customer in town, Terry"—and didn't want to get schnocked listening to the wife's banalities. The walk was pleasant. It gave me time to resign myself to the fact that there might not be any El Dorado. What scared me most was that I would slide back into my old way of life. I liked feeling vital. Independent. Heightened.

Terry met me at the door. They had called about Dad. He was dead.

My mother had died a number of years before, and poor old Dad had gradually slipped ever since. When he was seventy-five I put him in a nursing home. I wanted him to stay with us a few years, but Terry whined and bitched. Besides, all his friends were in Grosse Pointe—those who were left. He was okay at first, but then slowly declined into a very kind and gentle senility. I used to call him from the office every week. Eventually he didn't know who I was.

I flew out Friday morning. The nursing home was nice enough to make all the basic arrangements. I guess that's part of their service. There were a couple of his old friends who met me at the airport. I almost felt sorrier for them than for Dad. It was a terrible reminder of their own frailty, as well as their loneliness. I stayed at a Ramada Inn. There would be a lying in at the funeral home that night, with the burial next to Mother the next day. Funerals were not my favorite subject, but there were times when things had to be done right.

I was surprised at the number of people who came by the funeral home. There were Dad's friends, as well as the rank and file of the Ford executives. Even the Prince himself stopped in for a moment. I liked his style. A few nice words, a pat on the back, the shake of a few hands, and a quick departure. Sadly, it was probably one of my father's grandest hours.

About eight-thirty the last of the mourners had left, and I found myself standing next to the funeral director. He told me they would pick me up at eleven and that everything else was taken care of. I thanked him, and he left. I then walked into the room where Dad was laid out. I had avoided that all evening. He didn't seem very natural, despite all the rouge and hair spray. I couldn't so easily forget the babbling conversations of the past several years. For some reason, I wept, openly. Half my life was gone, and now too the man who had been so kind to me. The outings, the ballgames, the cheerful calls at exam time, the little extra cash when the boys were born. I knew it was time for him to go, but I wasn't really ready. He was all that was left of that era. The last reminder of the first half of my life.

The next day was much pleasanter. The sun shone brightly. I had asked the old friends to ride with me and to be pallbearers. The service was graveside—no one wants to be inconvenienced by having to go to both the church and the graveside these days, it seems. The minister—Dad was a Presbyterian—gave a short and very beautiful service. It was over in ten minutes.

I said goodbye to all assembled. A number of high school chums were there, much to my surprise. I had forgotten how considerate people were in the Midwest. A couple asked me to dinner—they *all* asked where Terry was—but I declined. I wanted to catch an evening flight out after a brief discussion with Dad's lawyer. It was nice of them though.

The lawyer met me at the Ramada, and we discussed the estate. There would be about three hundred thousand after taxes and costs. Half of that was to be given to various charities, and the rest was mine. I knew that. We had discussed it. Dad was the old-fashioned type who believed that the goal in one's life was to live comfortably. The balance of one's success was meant to help enrich the lives of others—or for the glory of God. It was an old Calvinist idea. I apparently lost it somewhere along the highway—along with the rest of my countrymen.

After the lawyer left, I called room service and ordered a bottle of Scotch. It's not every day one's father died and I felt I deserved a few good belts. I also ordered a hamburger—it was a Ramada, after all. When the bottle arrived, I poured a big one and sat in the silence looking at the frozen swimming pool. Next summer it would be filled once again with kids and lovely girls in bikinis. Life would go on. And, after all, there was a hundred and fifty thousand coming my way. Can't sneeze at that, even though it seemed like chicken feed just a week ago. I let my head slide down to my hand. Was I down! I felt like crying. All I had left were the boys.

I stood and walked toward the telephone. I wanted to talk with them. I hadn't brought them along because it was in the middle of the semester. But I wanted to hear their voices. I wanted to say something to them about their grandfather. He deserved it. They were his only living memorial. Just as I reached the phone, it tinkled. I picked it up, and the operator connected.

"*Poor baby!*" She moaned loud and low, causing my hair to stand on end. "Left all alone, isn't he?"

Revulsion, then anger, welled up inside as I encountered

such tremendous disrespect toward my father. I had the urge to hang up.

"Listen, you cocksucker!" I shouted. "Have a little respect, will ya?" The man's been in the ground for only two hours!"

There followed a silence, during which I could feel myself shake. Finally She replied in a high whisper. "Everything's going to be all right. Godmother's going to make everything all right. She knows how bad you feel."

Again there was a long pause, until I asked, "Why didn't I hear from you last week?"

"There was nothing to hear," she hissed. "Poor baby saw the figures."

"Yeah, but I've gone to a lot of trouble lately," I replied. "It's going to be tough as hell to make this thing work. We're going to have to have a little better communication."

During the next pause I could hear her breathing. It seemed forced, as if she had asthma. It was disgusting.

"That's why Godmother chose *you*, sweet thing," she replied, her voice modulating. "He's a smart little boy. He knows what to do. And he does what he's told."

This time I paused. I wanted so much to hang up, but I couldn't. I wanted back in the game. I wanted something to live for.

"Well, where do we meet?" I asked.

"Ooooh, in Chicago, of course," She replied before breaking into shrill laughter. "The . . . the . . . *Windy City*."

"Oh, Jesus," I exclaimed. "Can't we make it some place easier?"

"Oh, the little man probably needs to go out there," She answered. "He needs to visit his friends . . . where the action is."

"Okay, okay," I agreed, assuming she meant the Board of Trade. "Where exactly?"

"At the Field Museum," She barked. "You'll leave the book on a bench in front of the elephants Wednesday. At two o'clock."

"What happens then?" I asked, knowing She would want me to leave.

"You'll leave through the front entrance and walk to your rented car parked in front. You'll pick something up and return."

"Okay," I replied nervously, since I didn't know where the hell the Field Museum was. But I figured I could find it. Same for the elephants.

Again there was a long pause.

"And don't forget the *Winnie the Pooh*!" She screamed, hurting my ear. "Or the ten thousand dollars!"

"Ten thousand?" I asked, astonished. "Last time it was five!"

She disconnected, leaving me staring at the receiver.

Chapter 13

I WAS DISCONCERTED all week. Everything seemed to bother me. I had been ignoring my trading duties, and even got a minor rebuke from the chairman. I stammered some reply about the market's being inactive lately, but he just shrugged and walked away. He used to be a trader, you remember. Janet was having her period and didn't really want me around. Terry kept trying to make conversation during dinner—she thought the brooch signaled some new turn in our relationship. And I had to come up with the ten thousand dollars in cash for the Godmother.

I hated to do it, but I went to my bank and cashed a check for five. I timidly explained I was taking a trip and wanted to be liquid. Of course, the stupid cashier then spent ten minutes trying to sell me traveler's checks. The other five I got from Worthington. I told him I was going to Chicago for a regional sales meeting and wanted plenty of Playmate money. He got a kick out of that.

I arrived in Chicago Tuesday night late and stayed at the Palmer House, near the Board of Trade. I hadn't told anyone at the office I was leaving. I simply left a note for the secretary explaining I was taking Wednesday off for a physical examination. Terry got the same story as Worthington. It was dreary and lonely. I went to bed early.

The next morning I arrived at the Board of Trade and

had a meeting with a small, but successful local firm, well regarded in the industry for its discretion. I openly explained I was a bond trader in New York and wanted to open a secret account. I didn't want the firm to know about it because it would cost me my job. I told them I would soon be sending them cash.

I then asked the account executive to retire to the bar on the first floor for an early morning Bloody Mary eye-opener. Over the second one, I explained I was unhappily married and was supporting another lady in a rather grand style. Everything it took to support her was being paid for in cash, since I dared not risk evidence. The young fellow was rather impressed. He explained that the firm kept lots of cash around for their big customers: gambling, women, travel. If you got it—spend it!

I then walked to the nearest Avis and rented a car. I told them I would return it to the airport. I asked directions to the Field Museum, which was very easy to find. At 1:45 I found myself sitting in the front parking lot. I then experienced that old, godawful feeling. I had forgotten the goddamn *Winnie the Pooh*!

I rushed inside, buying a pass at the door. I hurried to the book stall at the rear of the Museum. Breathlessly I asked the girl if she sold *Winnie the Pooh*. Of course, I got a stare that would have discouraged St. Paul. I then grabbed a book entitled *Myth and the Believer* with a picture of a clay earth mother statue on the cover. The son-of-a-bitch cost seven dollars.

I hurried back toward the front and stopped suddenly,

realizing I was in front of the giant stuffed elephants. I hurriedly took the cash envelope from my pocket and placed it inside the book. Shame overcame me as I waited the final few minutes. *Winnie the Pooh* was perfect. Who the hell would steal a copy of that? But this book? Some wild, impoverished anthropological student might leap upon it. Oh, why was I so stupid? Why didn't I listen to Her?

At 2:00 I stood and walked out the front toward the car. It was as cold as Alaska, the wind coming straight off Lake Michigan. I sat in the car for a few moments, pretending to search for something, then ran back through the snow to the main door. Inside, I walked hurriedly to the bench and grabbed the book. A group of grammar school kids passed by noisily, so I rifled the pages looking for the piece of paper. I found it and froze, disbelieving my eyes. The figures were dramatic—M-1 up over four billion. This had to shock the market. It was going to be a really big hit.

Unfortunately, all the guessers were calling it sharply higher too. How lucky can they get? I called the commodity broker and told him to sell as many contracts at the market as the account would allow. He didn't like that, since it was contrary to his recommendation. The sentiment was already in the market, which was trading sharply lower. It floated a few thirty-seconds lower on Wednesday and opened an additional eight lower Thursday. By the end of the session that afternoon I had made about twenty thousand dollars. And sure enough, she called the figures exactly.

Friday morning the futures opened six lower and stayed there. I liquidated the account, realizing a total of about thirty-five thousand in the transaction. Needless to say, I was disappointed. After paying Godmother ten thousand, plus the commissions, I had made less than twenty in return. That was nothing compared to the time before. It almost wasn't worth it.

I was really tired by Friday afternoon. I went by the Racquet Club for a steam and massage. It made me feel better, but I was still exhausted. I guess I wasn't used to the tension She was putting me under. Terry had to go to a meeting, so I decided to stay at home and watch television. I cooked myself a hamburger and settled down with a drink in front of the tube. I tried every channel, but could find nothing but inane situation comedy shows. After the taxes I had paid and all the goods I had bought, couldn't someone have seen fit to produce *one* decent show for the audience above the third grade? I contemplated suing on constitutional grounds: equal protection for normal people. I switched off the television and looked for the Percy book. I couldn't find it, so searched Terry's room to see what she was reading. There was the biography of some ancient Hollywood actress, along with a book by Robert Penn Warren. Thanks, but no thanks.

I returned to the library and called Janet. Her voice sounded warm. We chatted about work. I told her I had been doing very well lately. I even told her I was trading secretly at the Board of Trade. She found that exciting. She was something of a rebel at heart. As I talked, my spirits rose. I found I could be intimate with her without fear of losing.

Eventually, she yawned and said she wanted to get to bed early. I asked how the period was progressing, and she replied seriously that the cramps wouldn't be alleviated until she had a child. My mind raced for a moment. A child. A new life. She paused and then said she would be leaving for the weekend. The way she said it, I knew there was another guy. She was being considerate. But it hurt like hell.

"Hope it's nothing serious," I said.

"God, no," she replied. "House party out on somebody's farm. Be back Sunday."

"I love you," I blurted.

"I love you too," she answered quietly, after a pause. "I'll cook you dinner Monday night."

The glow didn't last very long. Soon I was lower than ever. The liquor wasn't helping, but it seemed the only thing to do. I tried to think of a few old friends I could call, but there was none I really wanted to contact. I thought of the boys, but I felt that would be something of a role reversal. I found some classical music on the FM and decided to guts it out. Perhaps something would come out of a good mental cry.

They were playing the Mozart Requiem, and my mind wandered back to Dad. I told myself there was no reason to feel sorry for him. He had lived a full life. He was tired. Alone. But then I remembered there was no difference between him and me except for a few years. Why should the aging of the body set him apart? Stop his life? The simplistic slogans we spout about our aging parents don't hold much water. It's a disease like cancer, and just as embarrassing and painful.

My thoughts then turned to the Godmother. Had I truly ruined my life? I had certainly altered it. Never would I be able to forget I had done something fundamentally wrong. Even if I never went to jail, I had shown I was a whore. It was simply a matter of price. What would the remainder of my life be like? Would this haunt me? Would I some day be horribly humiliated? Old? Friendless?

My thoughts returned to dying. Suppose tomorrow I was told I would soon die? I had never contemplated such an event. Yet it happens to people like myself every day. And certainly one day I would get old like Dad. Helpless against the inevitability. With no faith. No one truly to love me—for whatever good that would do. What would I do? Where would I hide?

I pulled myself to my feet and stumbled toward the bedroom. It had turned cold in the apartment, and I was shivering. I had never felt so empty. So bared. I disrobed and crawled between the sheets. I felt myself curling up against the cold, my knees reaching toward my chin. I was frightened. I couldn't even comfort myself. And I heard a tiny moan squeeze from my face. And I felt my chest heave silently. Soothingly. And I sought the balm of sleep.

Chapter 14

LET'S STOP FOR a minute. Take a break. After all, we're here to enjoy life, aren't we? If not to be happy?

You must remember that despite the pain, those were extremely exciting times for me. When was the last time you had a supernatural visit? And I've grown to wonder whether pain is all it's built up to be, anyway. I mean, a toothache is *real pain*. Especially the sharp, nasty type. But it's not the stuff dreams are made of. Can you remember a really bad toothache from years past? Truly remember it? Where you were? What was happening in the world? When you talked with the dentist?

Yet think of your greatest piece of ass, if you'll excuse the vulgar. The one which was the most exciting. Which made your eyes water. I bet you can remember the girl's name. Every feature of her body. The color of the sheets. Her reaction when you moved inside. The lies you told afterward.

No, pain is definitely overrated. Probably because we go to such extremes to avoid it. In fact, we pursue pleasure with a good deal less zeal than we flee pain. Now that's silly, isn't it? The more one pursues pleasure, the less intense it becomes. Yet the more one resists pain, the less he enjoys comfort.

Don't get me wrong. I'm not espousing a new, oriental

solution to the human condition. I'm just saying that after forty-some years of running from pain, I wonder whether it was worth it. Or rather, whether I was missing something. Or wasting something. I'm sure this puts me on the aspirin manufacturer's shit list.

No, pain, I find, reminds me—among other things—that I am alive. That I have a finger—a marvelous instrument—when it gets cut. Or that I have a conscience when it gets bruised. And that's something after twenty-odd years with Thunderthighs.

Speaking of Terry, I divorced her. Knowing she had the lowest pain threshold since Albert Camus—she used to cry at home if Lady Megabucks hadn't chatted at the benefit—I did my best to ease the burden. Of course, given my new disposition—stated above—I should have slugged it to her. But I believe in leaving each to his, or her, own particular vision of pain. Instead, I called Reuben and informed him I was moving out of the house. I further said I wanted to make it short and sweet—if that was possible. He asked me the grounds, and I said I had none. He asked if there was another woman, and I said no. In a fatherly fashion he asked what in God's name was going on inside my otherwise brilliant mind. And I told him I was bored. And fed up with the injustice; "fed up" being a different animal from pain.

I moved to the Racquet Club, tipping the manager a hundred dollars to screen all calls, visits, etc. I let Reuben break the news. He was instructed to offer her virtually everything. The apartment, the car, savings accounts, forty percent of my income. I kept the boat. I agreed to support the boys.

I haven't spoken with her since.

I also took a nice vacation. I went for a week down to Rio for the carnival. I won't feed you all the details, but suffice it to say, I went ape. I ate, slept, and drank, and I mated everything that came within four inches. I wore either my bathing suit or a pair of tight white pants and a silk shirt. At approximately four most mornings I could be found at some party, nightclub, or bar doing a pretty fair samba atop a table. Frankly, the natives loved me. I told everybody I was in the film business.

I also bought a new apartment on the East River. It was small, but had a nice balcony. I had it completely furnished in contemporary furniture. I even threw a couple of nice parties. I didn't want Janet to move in at this stage—neither did she—but she spent a lot of time there. It was odd having a kitchen which was actually in use.

And finally, I bought a dog, a bull terrier. I named him George, after Terry's nasty little father. He was a lot of trouble at first, but afterward we got along fine. He liked me, the house, the boat, the food, and the drink. In fact, nothing made him unhappy. More than I can say for the last roommate.

As you might have guessed, the biggest reason I was able to be so generous with Terry was my continued success with the Godmother. Each weekend She would call me with instructions for the next meeting. About half the time it would be in or around New York. For instance, one time we rendezvoused in the library at Yale. Another time at the Cloisters. Probably the strangest place was on one of the out-of-town trips. It was at Bookbinder's Restaurant in Philadelphia. What made it odd was that, given Her instructions, She had to be in the room. Of course, the place was crowded with hundreds of people, but it was scary knowing She was one of them. That is, if She was.

I'm not, to say the least, an excessively romantic person. Nor am I given to flights of fantasy. But the Godmother had cast quite a spell over me. Even after several months of contact with Her, I had no inkling of who or what She was. I didn't feel the *need* to know—as long as the money was rolling in. But I was developing a sense of curiosity, bordering on affection. Even at Bookbinder's, I was embarrassed to look around. It would have been like catching an old lady in her underwear.

I continued to speculate, of course, who She was. But every guess turned out to be wholly unlikely. For instance, She couldn't have been a mere cleaning lady. How would She know so much about me? In fact, that was one of the best clues. She always knew where I was and what I was doing. I thought maybe it was someone at the Securities and Exchange Commission. They kept tabs on me, as well as on most bond traders. But a SEC employee would have no more access to money figures than I. And surely, it wasn't one of the few compilers of the figures. It would be more likely that She was a little old lady with a wand than one of them. But it still intrigued me. And my mind kept asking the question.

And my sense of well-being returned, slowly. I decided I wasn't going to go to hell, or to jail. I still felt a very strong sense of risk—it *could* have turned into a horror show of indictments, trials, and prisons. But something told me it wouldn't. I had faith in Her. As smart as She had been, I felt I could relax.

And I guess She could sense the same thing. Every time She called, She would inquire about the domestic situation. And the kids. Hell, it was becoming old home week. But that's a pleasant way to do business. It's the way the Southerners do it.

And did we do well! I say "we"—I was still putting ten thousand dollars in little *Winnie the Pooh*. That is, until she went to fifteen. I half expected a raise, but was truly disturbed by the amount. Nobody deals in fifteen thousands. We think in terms of ten and twenty. Even twenty-fives have crept into our decadent Western, rounded-off mentality—twenty-five being one fourth of one hundred, you see. But I didn't let it bother me. I was grossing over fifty a week. It's the truth. Truly remarkable. It almost got routine.

But it was very hard work. Not only did I have to juggle accounts between Worthington, the old guy up the Street, and the firm at the Board of Trade, but I also had to do my regular job. Of course, that was made much easier with Her help. I really didn't have to do much thinking. I just traded occasionally with Her figures and kept the house account doing well. The chairman got off my back and went back to believing I was Captain Marvel. But still, it was hard work.

On those nights when Janet couldn't make it over, I would start a fire in the fireplace and sit back in my new leather wingback chair—rubbing ol' George's back, naturally—plotting my escape. I figured with a couple of million I would be satisfied. And that I would leave New York and go some place warm. Florida maybe. Or the American Virgins. Any place outside the country. Brazil or Mexico or Southern California was out of the question. I also worried about my personal life. Who would be a companion? I knew Janet was there—and the merger was improving—but I decided to leave that until later. Life had had a way of handling such situations so far.

Now do you feel a little bit better? Did the break help? Everyone over forty needs an escape occasionally. But don't fret. We'll return to the action.

Chapter 15

SHE RAISED THE PRICE to twenty. I didn't argue. After all, She deserved something for what She provided. But I did plead with Her not to go any further. Getting that much cash together was almost impossible. Any larger amounts would certainly raise suspicions.

She merely hackled and mumbled something about the elves' new shoes. It was the first time I felt like telling whoever was on the telephone that She could cut the god-damn kid stuff.

Twenty thousand was going to be a *real* problem. I was currently getting five a week from the firm at the Board of Trade, plus five from Worthington. He was suffering under the delusion it was a tax-evasion scheme and kept reminding me his firm *had* to keep records. It was a convenient method of keeping his little mind occupied, so I neither confirmed nor denied his theory. The other five had been difficult. Each week I had to piece it together from a variety of sources. I'd cash a fifteen-hundred-dollar check here and a five-hundred-dollar check there. The gamblers would have been a good way to do it, but I was afraid that would open up newer and potentially more troublesome exposure. They're not the nicest people in the world.

I finally decided to solicit Janet's help. I figured she could somehow be good for part of the new five thousand. I thought about it for a long time, then made my move one night after a marvelous workout at the apartment. Janet, George, and I all lay panting in the bed. No one was saying a word.

"I need your help," I said matter-of-factly, reaching for a sip of cognac.

"How's that?" she replied, barely lifting her eyelids.

"I want you to become my partner," I answered, before spitting up the cognac, upon realizing it sounded like a proposal.

Her eyelids shot open wide, and she said, "Whaaaaat?"

"Business," I blustered, sitting up. "Strictly business. Well, not totally business. I mean, I wouldn't have asked you, if there weren't something more . . . more tender . . . involved."

Ol' George raised his head, looking first at Janet, then at me.

"I, uh, I need you to help with my futures trading," I said, the entire plan having crumbled in my mind.

"Ooooh, that sounds fun," she said, rolling over. "I like Chicago."

"Well, it doesn't involve Chicago," I replied, wishing I had come up with a better plan.

"Well, what is it?" she asked, shoving George on his side and slipping out of bed to get her robe.

Oh, remorse! How was I going to get her involved without spilling all the beans? Would she scream and run away? Would I have to tell her about the Godmother—all of it? I had made a serious miscalculation.

For the rest of the evening, she hounded me about the proposal. I kept fending off her inquiries, hoping to come up with a workable ploy. Finally it struck me.

"All right," I finally shouted, a big grin coming across my face. "Are you ready?"

"Why, of course," she replied, putting down the dish towel.

"I'm sharing the account with Joel Callicott over at Stern, O'Doherty. He's in the midst of a very nasty divorce and wants to get his share paid out in cash."

"So?" she asked, the quizzical look still not having left her face.

"I want to run the cash through your name," I replied feebly, wishing to God women wouldn't be so smart at the strangest times.

"Why not do it yourself?" she asked, her eyes narrowing.

We should never have given them the vote! "Because Terry doesn't know of my success, and *I* don't want her to get any records with which she could go to court for more alimony."

She stared at me a moment, and I felt like a schoolboy caught in a lie by his teacher.

"So you want the account in *my* name," she asked, tapping her lovely breast, "and *I'll* pay the cash."

"That's right," I gasped, realizing she was intoxicated with the idea of holding my money. They all want it, goddammit. They all want to get you by the balls. It's in 'em. They can't help it. It's got to be part of the primordial procreative process itself.

"How can you trust me?" she asked coyly, picking up the towel again.

I sighed with relief, sensing she felt it was just a "front" operation. "Because I love you," I replied, I guess because I knew she had both of them in her right hand. And she could squeeze anytime she wanted to. But she didn't—not then. She walked over and wrapped her gorgeous lips around my face, grabbing my crotch for good measure. I decided to let nature take its course. George decided to bark.

And, so, well into the summer, my life went on as usual, pulling in between a hundred fifty and two hundred a month. Oh, the agony didn't cease. There were whole nights I couldn't sleep, wondering about the ethics of the situation. In fact, I worried so much—and worked so hard—I became almost numb. There was a subtle tension to the operation which wasn't evident at first, but took its toll in terms of a strange, newly discovered fatigue. I even went to the doctor to see if I had cancer or something. Naturally I couldn't tell him all the details—he might have referred me to a shrink—but I told enough for him to diagnose the problem as overwork.

I accepted the verdict and decided to take the boys to Europe. The trip couldn't have been more timely. The boys—especially the older one—had been very distant since the divorce. I don't think they cottoned very much to their mother's personality, but, after all, it was the only mother they had. And I guess they felt they had to protect her.

But the trip gave us a chance to be together—and for them to be together. We went to London, where we stayed at the Dorchester, saw plays, ate in good restaurants—they particularly liked Simpson's—and perused museums. By the time we left for France, they were in very good spirits.

Paris was particularly fun. I did things I always wanted to do, but couldn't because of Terry. We ate very late at far-off, offbeat cafés. We spent a delightful afternoon at the racetrack. I even took them to a pretty "educated" nightclub on the Left Bank. I found out they were interested in the same little numbers I was. And that was somehow encouraging—these days.

Rome was something of an anticlimax. There wasn't much to do there but eat, or shop. We probably should have gone to Venice. I've never been there, but I understand the effect of the water is better than Disney World. Next time, maybe.

But, unfortunately, there probably wouldn't be a next time. The kids were growing up fast. It would be just a few, short years before they too would be caught up in the rat race, however you define it. I felt sad that they would never know the excitement of a personality like the Godmother. For, surely, only the truly great minds—or the lucky ones—are offered such opportunity. And it caused me to stare at them at times, wondering what type of people they would turn out to be. Whether I was the right example. What they would think of me when I was well put away in the grave and they were sitting around the Christmas fireplace with their grandchildren, answering the question of what great-granddaddy was like.

But, as I said before, they were strange kids. No wonder. They had a strange father.

I was sitting in the bar of a delightful restaurant on the Piazza Populo. It was boys' night out. The concierge at the Hilton—the only Hilton in the world I've ever been able to recommend—had suggested I eat there and then have a drink about ten at the bar on the corner. After two weeks with the sons, I was having trouble walking. Apparently the clientele at the bar understood such maladies in a most delightful and decorous fashion.

I had just finished eating a wondrous meal consisting of pickled artichokes, followed by boiled beef and spinach, when the waiter informed me someone had called.

I wasn't surprised She knew where I was—I had grown accustomed to that—but I was shocked She could master the Dantean tortures of the Italian telephone system. Simply put, I had discovered there wasn't a system.

Anyway, I remember walking toward the cloakroom thinking I had discovered a new clue to Her identity. She had to be the director of the CIA. Might as well blame it on him. Everything else is.

She screamed with delight when I addressed her forthwith on the line. In fact, She cackled for several minutes in a low, new sound. I felt a shiver. It brought me back to reality.

"Has baby had a nice rest?" she hissed, finally.

"Yes, I have, Godmother," I replied, with all the dignity I could muster.

"Is he ready to go back to work?" She snapped.

"Listen, I'm only human," I argued. "My work is tough as hell. You ought to try it for a couple of weeks!"

There was a long silence, during which I knew I had pissed Her off. I didn't want to do that. I only had a few more months and then would be able to escape. "Aw, come on," I said. "Don't get mad. Let's get on with the work at hand. Where are we going to meet?"

Again there was a long silence, and I remembered early experiences of Her uglier—potentially murderous —personality. My spirits sank immediately. I wished I hadn't come on the trip.

"Twenty-five thousand," She whispered. The connection was so poor I couldn't understand at first. "Twenty-five thousand," She repeated, chuckling as if to some insider's joke.

"*No!*" I shouted, startling the cloakroom girl. "I'm fed up with this! It's not going to be one penny more! I'm sick of it! You're . . . you're . . . demonic!"

The silence that followed didn't bother me at all. I *was* sick of the whole thing. I was sick of the perverse atmosphere which surrounded it. I was sick of the legal questions. To say nothing of the moral. "*No!*" I shouted again. "It's staying the same!"

"The child feels . . . apparently," She replied, in a perfect soprano, "that Godmother has not been fair."

"Fuckin' right," I answered, worried the Italian girl spoke English.

"Then, fine," She replied, reverting to the hiss.

We remained silent for a few seconds, only the crackle of the line filling the void.

"Where do we meet?" I asked again.

"Next Tuesday evening at Carnegie Hall," She answered, Her voice turning distant and sad. "Leave *Winnie* behind the ashtray next to the first hat check."

"Fine," I answered, confidently. "Have a nice evening." I hung up knowing I had reached a new plateau. There was a new understanding. It would be easier.

Chapter 16

J ANET?" I ASKED absently.

"Yeah," she replied, struggling to adjust her blanket without disturbing the delicate balance of the skirt pulled just below her bikinis.

"Did you miss me on the trip?" I asked.

"Sure," she answered, still struggling.

I took the wine from the portable cooler and refilled the glasses. A gust of wind made the blanket flutter. "Shit," she whispered.

"I . . . I want you to move in with me," I said, taking a sip of the wine.

There was a long silence, during which the sounds of the distant traffic could be heard above the rustle of the trees. Finally she rolled to her side, taking off her sunglasses.

"We're doing all right, aren't we?" she asked.

"Sure," I answered. "But why don't we make it a little more . . . permanent?"

"Well," she started, sitting up and pulling down the skirt, "I don't know if . . . if I can work everything out right now."

I paused for a moment, not wanting to rush things. "What do you mean?" I asked.

"Oh, Bobby," she said. "You know . . . I've been . . . seeing this guy."

"Well, I knew you were seeing . . . *guys*. Who's this?" I asked, knowing I was on dangerous ground.

"Well, what do you want to know?" she asked, staring at the sandwiches.

"Well, who is he?" I stammered.

"His name," she began slowly, "is John Buchanan. He's a . . . student, you might say. He's finished his architecture. But he's still studying. Art. He thinks it's important to architecture. Sculpture—things like that."

"Where's he from?" I asked, unable to think of anything else.

"Oklahoma," she replied, after a pause. "Tulsa, I think. Or someplace like that."

"How old is he?" I asked quietly.

She paused and then answered, "Twenty-five."

Goddamn, I thought, she's involved with a younger man. "Is . . . is he handsome?" I asked.

"Gorgeous," she gasped, her head sinking to her knees.

Well, there I had it. *Sex.* With some young punk hippie. And all along I thought there was some old beau or a guy who made her laugh or simply someone like *me*.

We both sat silently, surveying the remains of the picnic. A monarch butterfly settled on the cheese.

"You have to give me some time, Bobby," she said surprisingly. "I want horribly to move in—and I will. But this other thing'll take a little time."

"I'll . . . I'll take the risk," I blurted. "I want you more than anything on earth."

"Okay," she shrugged before turning full square toward me. "But we'll have to be patient."

It was a delightful evening in New York. A cool front had moved through, cleansing the air and reducing the temperatures to human levels. Even more delightful was the program at Carnegie Hall. Andre Watts was playing the Mozart Piano Concerto no. 20, one of my favorites. I don't want to give you the impression I was a serious intellectual; I'll leave that to the other bond traders. But I have always liked music, classical music, and was never able fully to enjoy it with Terry. She would go to Philharmonic night at Lincoln Center because that's what all the other Swells did. But Carnegie Hall? Or some lesser palace? Never! It's what all those *Jews* did!

Well, Janet, the Jews, and I had had a wonderful several months. We went to places in Brooklyn I didn't know existed. I heard people and music I had only known from records and radio. And I discovered I was a good listener. I enjoyed it immensely.

I left *Winnie* where I was instructed and we took our seats in the fourteenth row, center. One nice thing about being rich—you can afford the best seats. The program was magnificent and propelled me from all my concerns and anxieties. I even stood to cheer the pianist after a superb performance. During intermission, I walked by the ashtray and discovered the book was gone. At first I was afraid someone else had taken it, but then it occurred to me She was there. Surely She would stay for the performance. Why otherwise would She have suggested it? During the second half of the concert, I found it difficult to concentrate on the music, even though it was Mahler's Second. The fact She liked music told me more about Her than anything outside the money supply figures. She must have been someone of some background or education. Perhaps She was of foreign birth. All those Europeans love music, you know. But the best part was the realization that if She loved music, She couldn't be all that bad. I had nothing fundamentally to fear. At least She wouldn't kidnap one of the kids.

I returned to the ashtray following the applause and found the book. It was getting a little tattered from all its use. I had once thought about buying a new copy, but I decided the old copy was less likely to end up in the wrong person's pocket.

And the surprise inside was the nicest gift I think I've ever received in my life. Better than the sled when I was eight years old. Or the first back-seat rumble with Sarah Nixon when in the eleventh grade. The figures were up over five or six billion. With the new oil prices and the recent predictions of an awful winter, the bond markets were nervous. Furthermore, a brother trader at the competition had called me Monday asking if I could take a lot of stuff from him that week. I didn't do it because I basically didn't give a damn. But I was surprised to hear him say nobody would help him out. Apparently, the whole Street was long bonds. It had all the makings of a fantastic crash. And I could see myself short in this new financial *Götterdämmerung*.

Sure enough, the next day the markets were totally unprepared for a massive increase in the money supply. In fact, they were calling it "lower." The situation had all the marks of fabulous disaster. I went to work immediately. There would be a lot to do. I would maximize each account. I would even open a new one, somewhere. This was the really big hit I had been waiting on. Three, no, four hundred thousand. A half million wasn't out of the question. It could even turn into something bigger. I had to remind myself constantly to remain calm.

And it was grueling work. I had to reach each of the accounts—including the new one under Janet's name—and tell them to sell the maximum. There were protests in each instance. They were all expecting a mild rally. And, besides, no one liked the way I shot everything on a "hunch."

At noon I left the office and walked down the Street to yet another large commodity firm. It was risky, but I needed more access. What I was doing was totally illegal, even by the Board of Trade standards. I would be short well over the six hundred contract limit. If any of the various houses discovered that fact, they would shut me down. I opened the new account in my own name with my own social-security number. I wrote a personal check and told them to clear it through bank certification. It seemed almost reckless. I wanted to trade bonds before three o'clock. They agreed reluctantly—the idiot salesman didn't know what I was talking about—and by three o'clock I was short a hundred contracts in the account.

By five o'clock I was so hyper I could hardly talk with

Janet. She knew I had her position to the wall, but she still didn't know why. Finally she asked me what the matter was, and I told her—in a torrent of words and thoughts. The market was primed for a tremendous selloff. Never, in my ten years of successful trading, had I seen it like that. The question was not one of direction, but one of intensity. It could start a major bear move.

I remained quiet through the dinner and then during a terrific play on Public Television. I can't even remember what it was. All I could concentrate on was whether or not to make this the final plunge. I had seen a lot of guys in my day let fortunes slip through their fingers because they kept playing. I had a little over a million-one in the various trading and bank accounts. I had tax spreads which would render all of it capital gains. If I were to hit a half million—or more—the next day, I could walk off with as much as one and a half million free and clear. I had always said two million was the goal, but I could always trade carefully for the next several years on my own. The clear thing was I wanted to be rid of two influences: the firm—or *any* employer—and Her. She was getting greedier and greedier. Furthermore, She was the one exposed to criminality. To getting caught. Yes, I had to get out. The question was how and where.

Even the liquor couldn't calm me down. I was absolutely manic. I then knew what it must be like to win the Olympics or be elected President of the United States. Finally I had to put on Vivaldi's *Four Seasons* and lie in the middle of the floor. My heart was pounding dangerously.

Janet later had her own way of calming me down, and it wasn't a cold shower. It started, in fact, with a hot shower. I knew exactly what she was doing, and I felt like the young warrior being rewarded by the grateful princess. She put on rock music and then started with the soap. I've never seen so much lather—or frenzy. I went berserk—and so did she. Why hadn't I been doing *that* for the past twenty years?

The final elixir came in the form of a total body rub—interrupted at least twice by nature—with the help of something called Jergen's lotion. I was asleep by eleven. And I slept the sleep of the young and the virtuous and the carefree.

The market kept sucking higher most of the morning. That pleased me, in a way, because it would make the downward reaction much stronger. I kept looking at the faces of the other traders. Poor bastards. Not one of them had an inkling what was going to hit the fan at four o'clock. I couldn't resist helping one of the new boys. It was like knowing the Japs would be hitting Pearl Harbor. He didn't really know me, so when I told him about eleven not to get too long, he smiled weakly and began arguing. I let it drop.

Eating lunch was out of the question. Besides, I wanted to be alert to trade the firm's account. I know this sounds awful, but I wanted to use their long position to push the market lower. That still makes me feel bad. I took a walk instead. I even went over to Trinity Church, not to pray, like the usual crowd there at noon, for help out of a trading hole, but because I had never been there. It was quite peaceful. The rector even asked if I wished to pray.

I'll skip the drama. She fucked me. The figures were basically "unchanged." Nothing at all like what She had said. I knew why immediately. She was teaching me a lesson. Or else cutting off the relationship. But that was totally irrelevant at the time. The market was rallying. By five o'clock I had lost over seven hundred thousand dollars. And I had no confidence what would happen with the futures the following day. It could have—at perhaps the best—taken everything I had. The question was whether or not I would go far into the hole. And that could have been surmounted, except that the truth of my enormous trades would surely become public. In short, my entire financial career was on the line. It was the most dreadful moment of my life.

I didn't have the mental capacity to think about Her that evening. The question was one of survival. And one is never very attractive under those circumstances. I left the office reluctantly—afraid the others would notice my convulsions. And I *was* convulsing. Very near to throwing up. I didn't know where to go. I didn't dare go to the apartment. The thought of those four walls—Janet with her questions—the possible telephone calls.

Instead I went to the club. And not the steam room. I didn't think my pores could stand any further ventilation. Instead I went to the sleep room. And I lay there for over an hour moaning softly. Thank God no one else was there that late. I can't even remember what were my thoughts.

About seven I descended to the bar. Some asshole tried to make conversation, and I had to tell him I was ill and wanted to be alone. I drank, heavily. That was all I knew to do. All I could feel was sinking. Sinking so fast I had to grab the sides of the table. It got so bad I went to the dressing room and lay down on one of the leather couches. All was very quiet and dark. All I could sense was the rage roaring inside my head. I finally did vomit. But I didn't care. Somehow—shortly thereafter and through the grace of God—I fell asleep. And I didn't wake up until six-thirty the next morning.

Chapter 17

THE NEXT DAY was perhaps my finest. Oh, I took my beating. In fact, it came close to disaster. But only close. I survived, and I'm rather proud of the performance.

My greatest problem, in retrospect, was one of communication. I would have to deal with at least ten people: the brokers at the various firms I was dealing with; the guys on the floor; and, in one case, a principal at a firm who panicked when he discovered they weren't very well margined. The telephones at the office were out of the question. I had to have three lines open and be on one of them almost constantly. Even the coffee lady would have guessed something was wrong if I had all that going on in my little office.

Out of desperation I settled for the phone system at the club. They had four lines and a full-time receptionist. After four cups of coffee—and, frankly, a brief prayer which began, "Dear Lord, I know you don't owe me much"—I walked to the receptionist, a fifty-five-year-old rock of Irish respectability, and placed a hundred-dollar bill on the countertop. I explained I was under great pressure; that my whole life was flashing before my eyes; and that I had to know that someone would help me in my hour of need. I tried to well up a tear but, honestly, the source was depleted.

Her great breast swelled, as she shoved the bill toward me, saying, "A fine young man like yourself needn't seek help but through the Lord Himself and the simple request to an old mother."

"You are blessed among women," I mumbled, suddenly fearful she would take that as a blasphemy. But she didn't. We both let the hundred dollars rest on the counter, as I gave her the instructions. I was going to be in guestroom D for the entire day. I would be using two, maybe three, lines. It was vital I had her fullest attention. She nodded knowingly and motioned me toward the elevator.

The calls began immediately. And the struggle was on. I knew I could easily get to the floor through Worthington's firm, so I called him first. He started off with some sanctimonious horseshit about overtrading, until I had to cut him off short. I reminded him we could both get hurt in this matter. And his job was to service me, not hinder the operation. The floor broker knew the problem exactly—those guys have uncanny memories. He liquidated that account within five minutes at a loss I knew I could stand. I felt better.

The next operation went much worse. I contacted Janet's account executive and instructed him to liquidate the position. He was a prissy Yalie type and declared he couldn't "take instructions" from anyone but "Miss Quinlen." I informed him, in most florid terms, that if the account weren't liquidated immediately, I would not only hold him personally and financially responsible, but also drastically rearrange the architecture of the frontal portion of his head.

While he put me on "hold" to call his boss—or the police—I called Janet and got her on a three-way conversation. While she was complaining about my failure to come home the night before, I began screaming at her to shut up and listen. She got offended and threatened to hang up. I faked a sob—I couldn't have cried anymore if they had hung the First Lady in Red Square—and begged her to listen. At that moment, the Yalie got back on the line and began nasalizing. I said, "*Miss* Quinlen, please inform this *gentleman* that you wish to liquidate your entire account at the market!"

Well, Janet got confused, and I started swearing. The Yalie kept whispering willowy "My Gods," while apparently using sign language with his superior. Finally Janet caught on and said, "Well, if that's the way you want it, okay." That's not exactly the expression an account executive wants to hear when he's handling a ten-million-dollar position.

The delay saved us a few thousand dollars. The market dipped a point or so, as they were buying me in at a hundred-thousand-dollar loss.

The remaining accounts operated a bit smoother. The firm at the Board of Trade was almost exuberant—losses are great teachers, they kept repeating. The old man at the Street account was less appreciative of the circumstances. He didn't say much, but he continually gasped during the procedure, his cardiac voice growing fainter and fainter.

The rest of it was simpler. I no longer concerned myself

with profit or loss. The question was liquidation—to be out. And the lower the position got, the better I felt. In fact, I became almost euphoric toward the end. Because, you see, I *had* survived. I had lost everything—or almost everything—I had made over the past months with the God-mother, but I had not gone bankrupt. I would still eat. The kids would still go to college. Even Terry would be able to keep up appearances.

I stumbled toward the apartment around four-thirty and felt disoriented in the apartment. An hour or so later Janet made it home. She mixed a big batch of martinis and forced me onto the balcony. She made me wonder at the evening lights; at the stillness, even in that great city, which was mysteriously descending. She then forced me to discuss the play we had seen a week before at a little theater down-town. And it worked. I began to relax. I knew it wasn't a cure, but I knew I could make it until the next day. Then I confiscated the trick and began forcing myself to consider all those other things in life. And I was amazed I could do it—even if it were a self-deception.

Amid these mental meanderings came thoughts of Janet's artist-boyfriend. Snot-nosed little bastard, living off government grants and the charities of institutions. Stealing grown men's women—from men who needed them, who had nothing else. I thought of beating the hell out of him—or shooting him, in case he was of the heftier variety—in some dark bohemian stairwell. But experience told me it wouldn't last, that the glow would wear off. After all, he was probably a fraud—long hair and wistful, romantic statements about art mimicking nature. No, I would bide my time, hold on to this marvelous woman. Trust in basic truths.

I dreaded going to bed. I knew I didn't want to make love and that sleep was an impossibility. She knew what was wrong and turned on one of the late movies. Actually, it was pretty good: *Klute*, with Jane Fonda. I don't remember much after the opening scene. The next thing I knew, it was morning.

After breakfast the depression turned into abject fear. A funny thing happens when you temporarily get your hands on a bunch of money. It changes your entire personality. You become almost—and you won't like this word—aristocratic. Bourgeois concerns with money and morals become senseless. One rises to a higher plane, a greater purpose. But coming off that high can be horrific. And I could see how I had neglected my job. How I hadn't kissed the boss's ass lately. How I could be fired if some young hotshot happened along. And what would they do if they knew the truth? About the trading? About Her?

I sat on the balcony most of the morning. Trembling. I wished so desperately my father was still alive—and coherent. Surely I could have spilled the beans to him, even if it took a week to explain the technicalities—and he would have told me what to do, or how to act. What to do was not important at this stage—simply return to normal, friend. But how to act? How to treat this . . . this nightmare. After all, I had risked my whole life with a madman—or mad-

person—whom I didn't even know. I had never met . . . *It*! Didn't even know Its name. It was insanity. And I felt I was going insane.

Chapter 18

THE DAYS THAT FOLLOWED were unique to my experience. I never before realized what shock does to the body, or to the mind. Oh, I was able to straighten everything out. And, of course, I was able to resume my daily routine at the office. But it was several weeks before I was what one would term normal.

My eyes felt constantly strained, as if I hadn't been wearing badly needed glasses. My appetite vanished, and I lost ten or fifteen pounds. And I found my confidence almost completely dissipated. But perhaps worst was the shaking sensation I experienced *inside* my body. Inside, *everywhere*: the head, shoulders, arms, legs. I would look in mirrors to see if it were visible and see only the perfect picture of calm. But the shaking became so bad at times that I would have to return to the cubicle and shut the door. I didn't want anybody to notice.

And, of course, after a week of self-loathing and bitterness, I was able to shrug off the guilt. It was just one of those things that happen in life, I repeated to myself. Take it on the chin and go on living. Just don't make the same mistake twice—as if something like that ever happens twice.

And I was also able to forget my hatred for the . . . Godmother—I had a hard time continuing to use the silly name.

At one point I was convinced it was my duty to go to the authorities, but I talked myself out of it. I had done enough damage to myself. Besides, I never wanted to hear those awful sounds again.

There was a pleasant aspect to the recovery, however. And that was the fabulous sense of relief—as if I had been cured of a very long and painful disease. The realization that it was over was as refreshing as a large cold glass of freshly squeezed orange juice. It made me want to whistle at times. Or cry.

Janet continued to serve as my mainstay. Even though she didn't know all the gory details, she knew instinctively it had been devastating. And she remained by my side, constantly reassuring my fragile ego and diverting my attention when I concentrated too much on the past. She, like most women, seemed to be able to absorb the agony that we men are incapable of enduring. I used to think it was because they were dumb or because they couldn't fully empathize with the deeper hurts of a man. But after this experience I changed my mind, and their strange capacity took on almost mystical qualities. It was a force, an incredible strength that helped them ward off the evils of interior defeat.

Not that everything was perfect. She took a week off in late August to do her fall shopping and perfect her suntan. I came back early one afternoon, hoping she would be up for a few games of tennis. I burst into the apartment with such enthusiasm, it scared the hell out of her.

"Bobby!" she protested pathetically. "Please don't come

running in like that! This is New York. You scared the hell out of me."

Guilt blended with affection as I took her in my arms and held her face against my shoulder.

"I'm sorry, baby," I whispered. "It won't happen again. I'll buzz from downstairs. Say, I want to play some tennis. We can walk over to the Park. This time of day there won't be anyone there."

"I'm not up for tennis," she replied, moving away. "I've got to wash my hair. Besides, I've planned a big dinner for you."

"Oh?" I asked, just having recently regained my appetite. "What's that?"

"Home-made spaghetti—with the new machine," she answered, walking toward the kitchen. "With the garlic and proscuitto sauce."

"Fantastic!" I said, pursuing her. "I can go for a jog. It's such a beautiful day, I want to be outside."

"Okay," she replied. "You go jog and I'll run to the market."

I hummed as I walked toward the bedroom. This had all the makings of a great evening. My burdens felt lifted, and the air felt clean and balmy. I wished I lived in Florida where it must be like that all year long.

I took off my suit and shirt and quickly threw my underpants on the bed. I rummaged through the closet for my jock and shorts—the weather was nice enough to go shirtless. I remembered they were in the bathroom, so I walked toward the door. Immediately I knew something was wrong.

Water was on the floor. Not much, but enough. I stared at the glistening pools, one small confluence having begun to dry around the edge. One end of the tufted carpet was soaked.

I felt a compulsion to ignore the water, to pick up the jock and shorts, and leave the apartment. But I couldn't. I knew it was too important. The consequences were too immediate.

I heard the front door shut. She hadn't said goodbye, but perhaps that meant nothing. I took a large bath towel and threw it on the puddles. It sank gradually and turned dark. I then took my foot and finished the mopping. I took the dripping cloth and hung it over the shower rod.

The light was still superb as I left the apartment. I could hear the laughter of small children along the street. The flowers in clay pots were more brilliant than ever, as if intoxicated with the climax of summer. I began running.

It had been understood between us that the artist was around. And I felt that she probably saw him from time to time, especially since she hadn't mentioned a breakup. But why *my* apartment? And *my* goddamn shower? It evidenced a cruelty I didn't believe Janet possessed. But, of course, that wasn't her decision—a man just gets up and climbs into the shower after a sexual workout. It wouldn't occur to him to think about the poor bastard who owns the damn thing. Or the water and the damp towel.

The jogging felt good, I told myself. And it was certainly

a beautiful day. Besides, it was part of the deal. But in my goddamn bed!

The dinner was exquisite. After the spaghetti came veal Florentine. The endive salad was crisp, and the wine light and dry. We talked about work and the shopping she would start in the morning. After dinner we sat on the balcony and sipped espresso and cognac. The river sparkled with moonlight.

Once in bed, I felt compelled to ask something. To hear some response which would ease my fears. For I was afraid that his youth and his body would take her away from me. Every time I started to speak, however, I stopped myself. It was too soon. It would somehow break the rules. It was an intrusion.

I lay a long time staring into the darkness. I could feel that she too was awake. Fortunately, the air-conditioner was humming, providing us with a barrier. At some point I finally fell asleep.

Over Labor Day Janet was gone; she was visiting her parents. So I packed up and went sailing for four days. At first I was afraid of being alone, but I soon found out that a group of fairly patient seagulls could make pretty good company. And the effect was what the doctors ordered. The sea cleansed me of my introspection and set me calm.

One day I took along the son of an acquaintance. It felt odd being around such innocence. It made me wonder when it had vanished in me. I searched my memory—something I hadn't done for a long time—trying to rediscover some point in my past when I had been the same. I had a hard time remembering the teens. Oh, I recalled certain events—the enormous ups and downs, at least—but I couldn't remember that certain absence of guilt which is common to all children. After all, they have nothing to feel guilty about, being unable to commit any true transgression.

And those thoughts helped me return to the overriding question I had heretofore been unable to face. Did I deserve what had happened to me? Was there a justice in life which prohibited the wrongful gain? Which punished the too-easy? Is that not something reserved for the truly innocent—the children—and their Tooth Fairies and Santa Clauses?

But, after all, I never heard anyone criticize Henry Ford for inheriting a billion dollars. Or Winston Churchill for his three-hundred-year-old name. Or Andrew Weyeth VIII for his genes. Were those fellows wrong to take something for nothing? Especially since it wasn't offered to every peon or serf or Afro-American in the twentieth century? Let's face it. Behind most great successes is a great success.

But that still didn't answer the question. There seemed to be some *rule*, some law of nature, which had been evidenced. We're here to suffer, to find our happiness in the satisfaction of having fought the good fight. Should I resign myself to that? And, if so, what would I do next?

The days following, most of my sailing was caught up struggling with those questions. At one point I was going to quit my job and head toward Idaho where I would build a small lodge and concentrate on hunting, fishing, and honest work. Then I was going to continue with the firm, but simply to enjoy the intellectual side of the game. And finally I decided to take a year off. Merely to sit around the apartment and think great thoughts. Maybe try yogi. Smoke marijuana.

All that changed on the last day of sailing when I took along an old man who had the motel room next to mine. He and his wife had been coming there every Labor Day for years before she had died. And he kept coming, finding it the place most perfect to recapture the memory of their lost intimacy.

And—just as with the boy—the old man evoked odd ruminations. He too sat in the front of the boat, seemingly content to stare at the waves. And he too manifested an air of innocence—or, if not innocence, the aura of having paid his debts. So I finally asked him, straightaway, if he had ever done anything wrong. Naturally he didn't understand the question, so I rephrased it. Had he ever received something for nothing?

"You mean the free-lunch question?" he asked immediately.

"No, no," I replied with disappointment. "Can you *take* the free lunch? Are you punished for it?"

"I guess so," the old man replied, his eyes misting over. "I guess so, son. That's a good question."

The weather was magnificent during the first part of September. Day after day it was bright and cool and gusty. It raised my spirits and brought back an optimism.

Janet too was much refreshed from her sojourn in Arizona. She seemed so energetic—so lithe—waltzing around the apartment. A change of pace works miracles for everyone. We spent several long, quiet evenings on the chaise longue on the balcony, simply holding each other and talking about the rather ordinary experiences we had had during the separation. I finally got the courage one night to ask her about the artist.

"Oh, *John*," she shrugged. "Oh, he's still around."

"Do you still see him?" I asked.

"Yeah, every once in a while," she answered.

"Do . . . do I need to worry?" I asked.

"Hell, no!" she answered.

"Is it . . . is it about over?" I asked.

"Oh, Bobby, please don't . . . rush me," she said slowly. "Just trust me. I'll tell you if something's wrong. Just trust me."

And that's when I started going back to the club and spending rather long afternoons playing squash and using the steam bath. Something told me my insecurity was the product of my experience with Her. And that experience was endangering my true interests in life. I had to return to normal—if you could ever call my previous life normal—and find the golden mean. I had to give both of us room. I had to let life take its own course. I had to have faith in others. I had to trust again.

Chapter 19

THE CHAIRMAN KNEW something was wrong. I guess that's why he was the chairman. For several weeks I could feel his close observation. Oh, nothing intimidating, unless you happened to be an absolute basket case. There was just the casual drop-by the cubicle once a day; the invitation to lunch every so often—always for some business purpose. And then there was the big question—over coffee. Why hadn't I been active in the markets?

And, of course, I felt as brilliant as a mud fence. There were days when I couldn't tell you where bonds were trading within a hundred dollars per thousand. It wasn't that I didn't care. I just didn't have the power of concentration. Or the emotion, the stuff one trades with.

I explained the lessened activity by saying there were great uncertainties. How more profound can one become? And then I feigned irritation and asked, softly, if there were grounds for the question. Hadn't I been right during my tenure as head trader? Hadn't I always kept the firm's best interest in the fore? And, finally, why was I being pushed to trade when all wise men felt moved to remain cautious? That did it. No more questions. I knew I had a reprieve of several weeks.

Part of my time was spent asking myself why I endured such bullshit. The nervous stomach. The ignominy of the subservience. Yet it wasn't difficult to answer. I had an ingrained drive—call it avarice, although I don't think that's the answer. It was an automatic response. Something created from hearing the many tales at Ford. From the efforts at Country Day football games. From the club tennis matches. The exams in college.

But who cares? I kept asking myself. You're screwed up, and they're screwed up. It'll all resolve. You're in control. Just hang on. You've got the rest of your life.

The younger boy was applying to colleges, so I agreed to spend a few days on a tour of various campuses. We drove from Amherst to the University of Virginia. It was rather pleasant, with the beautiful fall leaves and colorful football fever. It was the first time we had ever been alone for such a long time. Oddly enough, after several days I felt a great urge to tell him the truth—all the painful and terrible things which can happen to people in their short march through the years. But I decided that would be in bad taste. The boy had picked up a little polish at seventeen.

I also felt a compulsion to give him a lecture on sex. After all, what were fathers for? But every time I tried to bring up the subject, he seemed to cut me off. And I didn't blame him. He probably knew a hell of a lot more about it than I did—the mechanics, at least. And how could I explain how one could make a mistake with a wife as I did? It was his own mother, for God's sake. I remembered a similar ride with my own father. He asked me if I masturbated.

Naturally I said no—that's how astute he was. And both of us spent the next ten hours avoiding each other's eyes.

But it was still a nice trip. We stopped a lot at McDonald's hamburger joints. And drank beer in the Holiday Inn rooms. And I gave serious thought to his ideas of becoming a Foreign Service officer. And I tried my best to look like good gene material during the admissions interviews. I think the kid loved me. I was trying my best.

"It's all over," she whispered. "I think."

I knew what she meant, even though we hadn't discussed the matter in weeks.

"How do you know?" I asked.

"I can tell," she whispered again. "It's not the same."

"You mean the . . . sex?" I breathed.

"Yeah," she answered. "It was all so stupid. I feel almost ashamed."

"I hope you weren't hurt," I said.

She didn't answer, and I knew I was through with all my problems. The long passage was over. I felt I had been initiated into true adulthood. Life lay before me like a calm spring-fed lake.

Chapter 20

I UNDERSTAND BABY HAS had a hard time," She cooed. "Why didn't he *love* Godmother?"

I had a hard time composing myself. When the telephone had rung I had been trying to tie a black tie to go to a dinner party at the chairman's house. I was going to be late, but I didn't care. I had always dreaded that moment, which I unconsciously knew was inevitable, but I now felt relief. Certain truths would now surface. Resolution was now felt at hand.

"I . . . I want you . . . to be . . . *calm*," I started, carefully choosing my words. "Because there are several very important things I want to say. Things important to both of us. And I want a very clear understanding of what I want to say."

There was no response from the other end, but I could hear the monstrous breathing. The old shaking returned in modest force. I knew it was fear.

"The first thing is that you came very close to ruining my life," I began.

I paused a moment, anticipating a diatribe of some sort. But nothing happened.

"Second," I continued. "I'm not at all comfortable—and never have been—with my . . . connection . . . with you."

Again I paused, hearing only the erratic struggle. The

shaking was getting worse, as if I were standing in front of an open door in winter.

"Third"—and I felt myself almost convulse—"I will never have anything to do with you again. Ever! I don't like it. I'm not built for it. It's not the way I want to lead my life."

And again I paused, hoping—almost—She would respond, say *something*, so I could hang up in Her face.

"I'm . . . I'm just not strong enough for it," I found myself saying, "I . . . I . . ."

There followed a horrific silence. Even the breathing stopped. The memory of all the previous torture returned. The only relief was the knowledge—the necessity—that I should not return to the fold. That I couldn't and wouldn't do. I was going to stand my ground. To hear Her out. To see the thing through, once and for all.

Slowly, but very surely, She let out a smooth, high moan. Hold on, I told myself. You've got to do this! Just hold on! You can take it!

"You will do what I say!" She finally screamed. "You will do what the Godmother demands!"

It was the worst I had expected. It was going to be a battle. Don't hang up the phone, you coward! I screamed to myself. Be a *man*!

No, Godmother," I replied, hearing my own voice shake like a child about to get a whipping. "I'm not going to do it. We're through."

With a frightening rush, the voice reappeared, rising from low to high, then shouting, "You'll either do it or go to jail! They'll have all the information. The secret accounts. Trading above the legal limits. Everything! It'll ruin you!"

"But . . . but it'll ruin you too," I replied with a whimper. "They'll get you too."

"Me?" She bellowed. "Me? Who am I? How can you get a fairy? You've never seen one? Nobody's ever seen one? That's impossible!" She then broke into her godawful laugh, which lasted unendurably.

I felt whipped. I feared I *was* whipped. Then I felt suicidal. I couldn't go on. I just couldn't.

"Hey, look," I bleated, all my defenses having collapsed. "I don't know who you are or what you're after. But please leave me alone. You can find somebody better and . . . and more *trustworthy*. I can even give you some names. Lots of other guys to contact."

"Yes," She hissed. "But you're the best. Sweet baby's the best. And Godmother only helps Her best children."

I gave up. I would listen to anything. If only Dad were alive. If only someone were there who could help me.

"I . . . I don't even know your name," I said. "And I insist on that. Why need we go through all this fairy story stuff? Let's put the cards on the table. Who the hell are you?"

A grotesque silence ensued, followed by a low, vicious groan from the other end. I clutched the telephone.

"I want you to hear this," She said softly. "You will do what I say or you will be punished for the rest of your life. I only hurt you because you were naughty. You will never be naughty again. You've learned your lesson. You love Godmother. You won't let Her down. And She will take care of you. She will love you. And you will sleep like a child. Happily. Very happily."

"What do I have to do?" I asked, defeated.

"You will receive a package in the mail," she answered, Her voice returning to its normal volume. "Inside will be forms necessary for opening an account at the Winterthur Bank in Freeport, Grand Bahamas. There will also be a thumbprint on a piece of paper. You will fill out the forms and enclose all the documents in an envelope. You will then fly to Freeport on a gambling trip. The next day you'll proceed to the Winterthur Bank and open an account. It will be a joint account. Joint with you and your signature and the person who possesses the thumbprint. Absolutely joint. You will bring all the papers back with you and leave them at the Atlanta airport. I'll tell you where later."

"But what good does that do?" I asked.

"You'll instruct the bank . . . to open an account . . . with your firm—" She said slowly.

"Hell, *no*," I shouted. "That's the only job I've got! I can't do that!"

"You will," She screamed, causing me to lift the receiver from my ear.

We both caught ourselves for a few seconds, my mind racing as it hadn't during the past weeks.

"You can then trade the account at your discretion—as instructed by the bank."

I knew immediately it was a good scheme. But there was only one problem. One I knew I could never overcome.

"Yeah, but sorry, Godmother," I said with fullest confidence. "Baby ain't got no goddamn *money!*"

Again the agonizing pause. Agonizing for Her, I hoped. I had gotten the message across. I wasn't going to risk any further money. Otherwise, why not take off for Colorado?

"Don't . . . worry . . . about that, child," She whispered.

"You open the account, and the money will be sent."

"How?" I demanded. "*I* can't do it. I don't have it! You *lost* it!"

"You open the account, sweet thing, and She'll see that the money's there," She whispered. "After all, what's a Godmother for?"

I know what you're thinking. And what you're asking. I don't feel I owe an explanation. But since you bought the book, I'll give you one.

First there were the threats, which sounded quite real. She certainly knew a whole lot more about me than I knew about Her. Second, She was bankrolling the new operation. And I felt that was an act of rare generosity in this world. It might have even signaled a feeling of remorse in Her. But most important—and I know this was going to sound strange—I was lonely. Oh, not the ordinary loneliness —Janet provided the best companionship I had ever had. It was the all-pervasive loneliness I had felt without Her. Without Her omniscience. Her power. Once I had felt Her influence, it was quite painful to live without it. And the very sound of Her voice made me realize that. Now life would return to the ideal. And I could return, perhaps, to the realization of my dreams.

I know you think I'm weak, and perhaps that's true. But I don't think it's your place to cast the first stone. Unless, of course, you've been through what I have. And you probably think me corrupt. I don't see it that way. For I had come to believe in the Godmother. Not as some kindly old lady one sees in the children's books. But I did believe She was a force greater than any other I had experienced. One we human beings have always looked for. And, therefore, what I was doing was fundamentally moral. Excepting the secret account, of course.

And last, I could perhaps find the answer to my question. Whether there could be the counterpart to Job. The man who is blessed senselessly. And lives happily ever after. We would see.

Chapter 21

THE NEW OPERATION went as smooth as silk. I flew to the Bahamas and opened the account. She called me that afternoon and said to return the next day through Atlanta, leaving the documents on the hat rack outside the coffee shop in the main entrance to the airport terminal. I followed Her instructions to the letter, arriving back in New York the same evening.

Several days later, the head of the foreign accounts department at the firm asked me to have lunch with him. We went to a swish little place in the fifties. He could barely contain his excitement when he told me about a strange new customer who had come to his department through a bank in the Bahamas. The instructions from the bank were quite unusual. The chief bond trader at the firm was to trade interest rate futures at the Chicago Board of Trade with full discretion. There was a half million dollars in margin money. And they were paying *full commissions*. I didn't remember telling them that!

I told him it was out of the question. First because it would interfere with my other duties. And second because it smelled like hot money.

"No, no," he insisted. He knew the bank well, and it was perfectly reputable. He said he had reason to believe the money was German.

"Well, what do I get out of the deal?" I asked. "It just means more work for me."

He offered to split the commission with me, which I thought was a nice twist. Although the Godmother might get a little pissed.

Well, after two cognacs, I gave in. But only on three conditions. First, no one in my department would know about the arrangement. I didn't want my traders to think they could all moonlight for the commodities section. Second, I was to have my own line and clerk at the Board of Trade. Third, no one in the firm was to know the results, except the two of us. He agreed readily and ordered a bottle of champagne.

Within three days I heard from the Godmother. She was rather sweet, praising me for the smoothness of the setup. We both chuckled when I told Her about the luncheon with the fellow from foreign accounts. I confessed the commissions split, and She laughed again. I offered to reimburse the account, but She pooh-poohed the idea.

I met Her the following Wednesday in the Student Center at Princeton. I brought along ol' *Winnie*, which had a new plastic cover. I left it at the hat stand while I went through the cafeteria line. After lunch, I went back to put on my coat and found some delightful figures. I knew there would be a big move.

The return to New York on the bus was strangely pleasant. I couldn't figure out why I was so happy riding through New Brunswick. And then I realized how content I was. Life *was* back to normal. I felt relieved. Protected.

I put on the maximum long position Thursday morning and went home that evening knowing it would be worth a couple hundred grand. The next morning I felt like a million, humming and skipping around the apartment. Janet was pleased, yet a little mystified by the sudden change in mood. I just told her I was happier than I had been in years. That life seemed to be working out for me. And that I loved her.

And so, week after week we followed the same routine. We met in some truly odd places. Longwood Gardens in Wilmington. The Statue of Liberty—first time I had been there. And even in a seedy hotel lobby on the Boardwalk in Atlantic City. And She continued to be pleasant—although every time I heard Her voice I trembled slightly. I could never forget the horrors of the past.

There were a few weeks when nothing happened, of course. But, in sum, we were still making lots and lots of money. And every week, as soon as the account was settled, the money would be transferred immediately to the Bahamas. By Christmas I guess we had close to two million dollars. The guy from foreign accounts thought I was Muhammad Ali, of course. But if he had any suspicions, he kept them to himself. After all, he was making a fortune on the commissions.

Janet refused to discuss marriage, yet moved further and further with me toward breaking down those immense barriers lovers erect between themselves. We both felt a strong individuality was necessary—like gravity—but we each wanted to be able to trust the other. To be able to express the affection we both felt. To be able to become vulnerable, childlike, with each other.

She changed firms after the New Year. The new job offered more money and a greater responsibility. It also meant longer hours. I was tempted to discourage her. After all, we would be traveling a lot, if she wanted to stay with me. I still felt I couldn't reveal the Godmother to her. I would do that later, when all the cows were home.

And I began growing plants. Now I know that sounds trite, but it provided a tremendous satisfaction. It too was something we did in joint venture. We liked them for the same reason. They were almost like pets. Or children. I took the role as authoritarian-softy. Never too much water! More fertilizer! She took the role of pusher-protector. More time near the window! Too much night light! It was a lot of fun. I was looking foward to the summer when we could send the "kids" to the balcony.

And I was reading more and listening to more music, usually at home. And we went to the ballet, something I had never done. I was taken with the athletics of the art. I didn't care if they were sissies. The combination of strength and grace overwhelmed both of us.

And there were movies and cold weather camping trips and, of course, the boat. Even in the winter, it was a pleasure to be near it.

And last, but not least, there was the lovemaking. It was like none other. Certainly none in my experience. It would be long and unfettered. Filled with tiny intimacies and laughter. Intent on success. Sometimes thunderous. At others, almost disinterested. Oriental. It would make up the most joyous and assertive moments in my memory. I would lie often, thanking God for my body.

In late January I decided to take Janet, and the boys, to Sun Valley for ten days to ski. Naturally I was worried how they would accept her, but I wanted them to know and like her. And to be prepared for the inevitable.

It was a little tense at first, but they soon realized what a warm, generous person she was. It felt rather odd, as I watched the three of them taking the lift together to the higher reaches of the mountain. They were actually closer in age to Janet than I. And certainly part of a generation different from mine. I wondered if they were physically attracted to each other. Whether I should be jealous.

The trip was a great relaxer. I needed the time away from the markets. Not that the Godmother, stopped, however. On the first Monday morning we were there, She called in the room and told me to leave the book in the men's locker room next to the outdoor swimming pool at the Lodge. Without giving it much more thought, I skied until Wednesday, leaving the book early that morning before going out to the slopes. That afternoon, when we all returned for one of those marvelous hot swims, I reached up and found the book with its message. The money figures were basically unchanged, and I remembered debating whether they would make us any money, as I slid into the pool.

Just as the waiter brought me my first drink, it struck me, however. How in God's name did She get all the way to Sun Valley? You practically have to charter a plane to get there. And that was the first clue I had to Her identity. She had to have an occupation that allowed Her to travel whenever and wherever She wished. That ruled out the cleaning lady or the chairman of the Federal Reserve. And it also meant She was a man. How else could She have entered the men's locker room? Unless She chose a time when no one was there.

But I quickly put those questions out of my mind. I didn't *want* to know who She was. I wanted Her to remain a mystery and a wonder for the rest of my life. I was rich and happy. With a beautiful lady and two nice kids. I didn't want anything to change.

Chapter 22

Y OU CAN'T IMAGINE my shock when I got the news. I could scarcely believe my ears. It left me stunned for several days.

"Why?" I had asked. "We've got almost four million bucks in the account. Everything's going so smoothly. We can just let it pile up. We can go on forever."

"No, no," She whispered. "Godmother must leave. She must return to the . . . Enchanted Forest."

"Have I done something wrong?" I asked, my voice cracking. "Are you unhappy with something?"

"No, no," She whispered again, Her own voice sounding sad, despite the hiss. "It's just that my work is done."

"Yeah, but what about me?" I asked, fearful She would hang up.

"You've done well," She whined. "You're well taken care of."

"Yeah, but . . . but I like it this way," I stammered. "I like talking to you. Knowing you're . . . you're there."

"Oh, Sweet Baby loves Godmother," She purred. "And She loves Sweet Baby. She'll miss him."

She then gave me the figures for the coming week. I barely remembered to write them down. I had one more week to convince Her to change her mind. I had to keep Her. She couldn't leave.

I became so morose I had to leave the office. I thought of going home, but didn't want to be alone. I went to the club and took a steam bath. There was no one there, but it gave me time to think.

Why would She want to quit when things were going so well? No, She wasn't trying to punish me this time. She really was going to disappear. And yet I had so much to tell Her. She, who had brought so much good out of what seemed evil. The order to my life. The softening inside myself. And, of course, the largess.

I went to the bar and ordered a Scotch and soda. I observed the other members, sitting in groups and chatting. What would they think if they knew my thoughts? Could I ever convince them I wasn't a fraud? Or insane? I had a couple more drinks, then left. I decided to walk home, hoping the cold air would clear my mind.

I passed by a window where they were erecting an Easter display, even though the holiday was still weeks off. And I saw the tiny white rabbits and colorful eggs and the reproduction of Mother Hubbard, her giant shoe lying in parts against a wall. Such was the stuff dreams and fortunes were made of. And goodness. And righteousness.

Janet arrived home somewhat late. She had an armload of things for dinner. I sat in the living room sipping a martini and observing the plants. She apparently sensed something was wrong and began fixing dinner. I appreciated her kindness and felt like crying.

Terry chose that point in time to start a ruckus over the child-support provisions of our divorce settlement. I refused to talk with her, on Reuben's advice, but it still upset me. She wanted more money because the boys were using her apartment as home base from school. The petition got rather nasty—which was probably shrewd strategy—and mentioned I was "living in sin."

Shortly thereafter I got a call at the office from Janet's father. I had never met the gentleman, nor his wife. He said he was calling because he and the wife had had enough of their daughter's involvement with a married man. I tried to explain I was no longer married, but he kept interrupting with phrases containing "two small boys." Even his voice depicted the paragon of the big business executive: tough, spoiled, moralistic. It took all the strength I had not to tell him to go to hell—being talked down to was the worst part—but I remained silent. He ended with, "Show me what kind of man you are, son! Show me you know what's right." I hung up. I should have told him about the artist.

I mentioned nothing to Janet about either situation. She had been so helpful to me, I felt I should bear those crosses alone. My bill from Reuben was going to be rather healthy.

I took all those events as an omen of the Godmother's leaving. The whole world knew, it seemed, I was departing Her aegis. I would be left as their quarry. At the mercy of the barbarians.

The last time She called I interrupted Her to plead for more time. I explained how my wife and my girlfriend's family were closing in. I knew it sounded stupid, but She couldn't leave. I could sense impatience, as She emitted a strong scream.

"Godmother doesn't want any *talk* from Sweet Baby!" She shouted. "She won't forget him. He'll be all right."

"Yeah, but it's not fair," I argued. "You can't just forget me the way you're doing. We're . . . *friends*. We've been through a lot together."

The depressions returned. I heard no more from Janet's father, but the wife's lawsuit had all the makings of a major vendetta. Reuben counseled that I resist to the end. I guess so—he was getting some handsome fees!

I became so distraught over the suit I called him one afternoon and asked for a meeting. He said he'd be at the bar at the Harvard Club at six. I told him it was quite important. I could think of nothing for the remainder of the day.

I was at the bar at five-thirty. I even decided to drink beer, so my mind would be orderly. He arrived at six and was greeted by a round of helloes from various other habitués. He spied me through his glasses and led me to a small table out of earshot. He ordered two vodka martinis—doubles—and lighted a cigar. "What's the problem?" he mumbled.

"Reuben, I don't want a new accounting of my personal financial affairs," I said.

"There's not much I can do about that," he said. "The judge will need to know what you earn at this stage."

"How thorough do they get?" I asked.

"They're going to get damned thorough from the way

you're talking," he said, thumping the cigar. "We're not going to hide anything from the court as long as I'm your attorney."

I was stopped dead in my tracks. I wasn't going to let anyone in the world know about the account in the Bahamas. If for no other reason than to protect the Godmother. I knew that game was up, so we chatted about our chances for a few moments, and I left.

I now knew what was in front of me. It was time to break and run. I didn't want Terry's attorneys poking around my records and revenues. In fact, without Her I didn't think I would enjoy living in New York playing the bond game. All I had was Janet and the two million resting in the account. That would be plenty. It was more than I ever dreamed of having.

So that was it. I would go along with the Godmother. Perhaps She even knew of all these matters. I was going to leave. They could levy what they wished against me. In fact, I would even settle with Terry for another thousand a month. I could afford it. I was leaving. And I would ask the Godmother to go with us. For I wanted to be where She was. That's the kind of life I wanted. I would go to the Bahamas and meet Her. Face to face. And then go to the ends of the earth.

Chapter 23

NOW I'M SURE YOU can understand my state of mind as the taxi labored over the narrow roads toward Freeport. I felt like telling the driver to hurry. But I knew She was aware of my progress. She seemed to know everything.

Instead, I laid my head against the seat and closed my eyes. There was much to do yet. After the bank I would have to go by the airline ticket office and book the flight to Zurich. There was a plane leaving every evening via London. I would book two tickets. Janet might object at first, but surely she would want to come. Especially if I promised a stay in Paris.

The wind wafted sweet fragrances across my face as the driver snaked through a small forest. It was necessary to relax after so much tension. I even let my mind wander. I wondered what She would look like. What age. Which sex. What we would say to each other. Whether She would agree to a more permanent relationship.

It took almost an hour to finish the trip. Once again I grew nervous as we approached the outskirts of the city. By the time we made our way through the noontime traffic, I was filled with anxiety. I tried to pay the driver, but he mumbled something about the bank. I tipped him five dollars American.

I walked inside, barely remembering what the building had looked like on my previous visit. I remembered the foreign business was done on the second floor, so proceeded toward the stairs. At the top, I gave the receptionist my name and took a seat.

Oddly enough, there was no one else in the reception area. It was lunchtime, and everyone seemed to have left. That was good, I told myself. Whoever walks up those stairs is my man—or woman. There's no hiding here.

Several minutes later a door opened, and a small, friendly looking gentleman in a white suit appeared. My heart pounded, as I rose to my feet. He walked toward me and extended his hand. With an enormous grin on my face I introduced myself.

"My name's Cullerton," he answered. "I'm president of the bank. Pleased to have you."

I don't know which was more painful, the disappointment or the embarrassment. I followed him meekly toward a small room. Inside he shut the door and signaled for me to take a seat in front of a large table. He then took one himself and began shoving documents toward me.

"If you'll be so kind as to fill these in," he said, "I'll be right back with you."

With that he stood and left through a second door. I looked at the documents and realized it would take me twenty minutes to fill them out. The Godmother must have been running late. But She would have to show up some time. After all, the account was joint, and She would have to appear simultaneously before they would give us our money.

I began filling out the forms, sweat beading on my brow. The day was becoming terribly hot, and the air-conditioning was insufficient. Suddenly the door from the reception area opened, and I jumped. I turned, and there standing in the doorway was one of the most beautiful black women I had ever seen.

"You're . . . you're the Fairy Godmother," I stammered, completely surprised.

"No, I'm the tea lady," she replied without a wrinkle. "Would you care for tea?"

Maybe she thought it was a joke, I assuaged myself, as I accepted the cup of hot tea. They must be used to odd people down here. I took several sips before realizing it would only make me sweat more. I went back to the forms. After fifteen more minutes, I was finished, and the president returned.

He took the forms and turned without saying a word. I cleared my throat and asked, "Hasn't the other party to the account arrived?" He paused and said, "Oh, yes, I'll check on that."

I waited perhaps three or four minutes before he returned, this time carrying an enormous satchel. He placed it on the table and pulled out a large sheet of paper. "Here is the accounting for the account, Mr. Reed, and the pouch containing the currency. If you'd be so kind as to verify the figures and count the money, I would be most appreciative."

Before I could speak, he began taking stacks of money

from the satchel. I gasped. "You did specify American, didn't you, sir?"

"Yes . . . yes, I did," I stammered, overwhelmed by the mounds he kept creating. I had never seen so much money in my life.

He left quickly, and I sat staring at the piles. It would take all day to count that much money. I would have to be satisfied with a rapid inventory. I quickly began grabbing stacks, thumbing through them like cards. After checking several of them I realized each represented twenty thousand dollars in twenties, fifties, and hundreds. And the bills were all new. There were over a hundred stacks. That's over two million. After checking at random another dozen I decided to take their word for it. They were a big bank with lots of foreign customers. They weren't in the business of shortchanging wealthy Americans.

I put all the money back in the satchel and zipped it shut. I hated to walk around with all that cash, especially in an official-looking container, but I had no alternative.

As soon as the president reappeared I asked him if I could have the satchel. He hesitated a moment and said it would cost twenty-five dollars. It was specially constructed, he explained. I pulled twenty-five from my pocket and handed it to him.

"Now, tell me," I said, standing. "Where's the other party. The one who's joint with me on this account?"

"Oh, you mean the old lady," he replied, turning again to leave.

"Yes!" I screamed, lurching toward him. "Where is She?"

"Why, she just left," he said. "She requested a separate room. Something about your being her illegitimate child. Didn't want to see you face to face. I felt it best . . . from your point of view—"

"Oh, my God," I gasped, reeling from left to right. "Which way? *Where's the room?*"

"Right there," he replied, pointing toward the second door. "But she's gone."

I bolted through the door and found a room identical to my own. There was a window, however, and I raced toward it. The view toward the sea would otherwise have been most picturesque. One could see lovely old colonial buildings painted bright pastels. And beyond lay the Yacht Club and harbor. I was about to turn away in frustration when I saw a figure limping markedly. It was a small, older lady in the distance, walking hurriedly with a satchel toward the water. Almost immediately She disappeared into a narrow street.

I turned and raced toward the door, suddenly remembering the money. I hesitated a moment and then returned to my room. The president stood with his mouth opened slightly, as I shoved the money into the satchel. "Excuse me, sir, but you haven't signed the accounting," he said. I grabbed the sheet of paper and scribbled on it. I then took the money and dashed through the door.

I almost fell down the stairs leaving the building. It was She! I was just a few feet away from Her! I should have said something. I should have known She would pull a trick.

The midday heat hit me like a brick, but I kept running. I rounded the bank building, the satchel swinging awkwardly at my side. I ran as fast as I could down the street where I had last seen Her. Once inside the labyrinth of small buildings I became disoriented. I finally had to stop a native and shout, "Where's the waterfront?" He pointed me down yet another winding street, and I took off. I was sweating profusely.

I finally arrived at the waterside and came to a stop. I looked first one way, then the next. There wasn't a soul in sight. I felt anger and then frustration well up inside me. Why did She run away? Why didn't She stay to say *something*?

At that moment I looked out toward the middle of the harbor, attracted by a noise which was the only sign of life. And there, racing toward an opening in the seawall, was the boat, the speedboat with the scuba diver. And I could see him standing at the helm, opening the throttle to full. There had to be a connection. She had to be on that boat!

I turned and raced back toward the bank. I needed a taxi, and bad. Naturally, they were all at lunch! I ran up one street and down another, stumbling in the heat like a madman. A few figures in the shadows stared at me, wondering what trouble I had incurred. I finally spotted a taxi—without a driver. When I arrived at its door, I began screaming, "Driver! Where's the driver?"

Soon a young native appeared in a doorway wiping his mouth with a checkered napkin. "Off duty," he mumbled through a mouthful of food. "Goin' take nap after lunch."

(157

I whipped a hundred-dollar bill from my pocket and shoved it toward his face. His eyes grew narrow, and he nodded. He disappeared for a moment and then reemerged pulling on a shirt. We both climbed in the cab and roared off.

Halfway out of the city I remembered I hadn't gotten the airplane tickets. I started to tell him to stop, but decided against it. I could always call from the hotel. What was important was to see Her. To find out the truth.

Chapter 24

THE DRIVER PUSHED his taxi like a madman, yelling at it and whipping the dashboard with his fist. I had upped the ante to a hundred fifty. The speedboat would arrive much sooner than a car, and I couldn't let Her get away.

And I was staggered by what I had seen. She *was* an old lady. Even the way She shuffled as She vanished from my view. It was unbelievable. My mind was in chaos.

The ride was terrifying. All of the children managed to get out of the way, but a couple of chickens didn't. There was a near miss with an old hearse, but I'm sure the mourners understood. People die everyday, but they don't always get to meet a fairy godmother. It wasn't until we hit the curves that I became frantic. The driver was now maniacal.

That's why—when the explosion occurred—I felt a mixture of rage and relief. I really didn't want to ride with the man any further. I wanted to live.

I clambered out of the smoke and haze, not knowing what to do next. The driver was frantically trying to put out the fire before it spread to the gas tank. I decided to seek safer ground. But just as I stepped to the middle of the road a motorcycle whizzed past my leg causing me to fall backward. I screamed at the white kid driving, questioning his mother's virtue. He came to a halt, and—like most rebels—stood stunned as I rebuked him.

"Are you headed toward Reeltown Bay?" I demanded, getting up and running up to him.

"Yes, I am," he replied, apparently thankful I wasn't dead, or wasn't going to hit him with the satchel.

"Give ya a hundred dollars for a ride," I panted, taking out another C note.

"Why . . . why, sure," he replied, grabbing the bag and putting it between his legs. "Get on."

I jumped on the back of the motorcycle and reached around the kid's waist. I decided to grab him and the money together. You see, I had never been on a motorcycle in my life, and I was sure those would be my last moments.

We took off with a lurch—I had shifted my weight in the fright—but soon began speeding up the hill. I didn't know the damned things were so fast! I knew I had made a very big mistake.

Sure enough, after we reached the crest, the damned fool began speeding down the other side. The roar of the engine and the wind were so great he couldn't hear my screams. I wanted to get off! I wanted to live! But he couldn't hear a damn thing I was yelling.

We finally reached a leveler stretch in the road, and I decided the journey was more important than the risk. So I closed my eyes and rested my head on his back. If I were going to die, I didn't want to see it. And for the next ten minutes or so, my whole consciousness was captured by a series of flying sensations. First up, then down. Next a sway to the left, which surely must have made us parallel with the earth. I just ground my teeth and moaned softly.

And then suddenly we came to an abrupt halt. I looked up at once and found myself staring at the side of the cement truck. I didn't let it phase me. "Drive on!" I shouted. "Let her all out!"

And that's what he did—I guess. I didn't watch again. I think I might have prayed. And time passed, my stomach becoming nauseated from fear. But I knew what I wanted. I wanted to see Her. I wanted it worse than anything in the world. I had to see *Her*!

When we arrived at the entrance to the resort I told the kid to drive straight toward the dock. "I can't do that," he protested. "They don't allow big bikes in here."

"Get this mother down that path!" I growled, trying to sound like his father.

We made our way through various walks, fortunately not passing any of the snotty personnel. We finally came to a barrier created by the elaborate bar set by the sea. I told him to stop and stepped off the vehicle. My legs wobbled underneath me.

"I gave you the money, didn't I?" I asked walking backward toward the water.

"Yeah," he said, somewhat dazed himself. "Thanks. That's really nice."

"You're quite welcome," I replied, before turning and forcing my legs to run toward the dock. Several guests turned as I passed. I knew I must have looked like hell. My hair was blown awry; my suit was covered with dust;

and I was shaking from the experience. I arrived at the path above the dock, but couldn't wait. I had to see if the speedboat was there. I charged through a stand of sea grape, frightening a young couple coming up the walk.

I shoved away the branches with the satchel and quickly scanned the lovely, innocent bay. And there, nestled next to the last pier, was the most beautiful sight I had ever seen. The speedboat was back, "The Treasury" painted on its stern.

I turned and stumbled down the path. I then began running along the dock. The satchel was growing heavy, and I felt awkward. But I didn't care. The odds were good She was still there. I reached the side of the vessel and threw the money aboard. I then carefully stepped onto the railing and sprung onto the deck. It was about to happen. I was about to meet the Godmother!

At first I hesitated. Perhaps I should be courteous, I told myself. After all, if She wanted to meet me, She would have done so at the bank. I stepped toward the closed hatch leading below. That's when I heard it.

I knew it was She. The animal sounds. The groans. The shrieks. It was similar to the other sounds, ever since the first day. My heart soared. She's there! I told myself. She may be some ugly old lady, a witch perhaps. But She's there. I'm going to get to see Her. Face to face!

With that I took hold of the brass handle to the hatch and began turning it. Everything held me back, but I knew I had to do it. I continued turning the handle, my whole being preparing for the vision awaiting me on the other side. And finally I could feel the latch give way. And I began opening the hatch—shoving it further and further—the animal sounds becoming clearer and clearer. Until, suddenly, the door was open. And the sounds stopped.

Confusion followed. It was dark inside the cabin, and my eyes struggled to adjust. Suddenly a male voice asked, "What the shit?" I stumbled down a short ladder.

Quickly my eyes adjusted and met those of Janet. She returned my stare for a number of seconds, then rolled her head to one side, with a soft "son-of-a-bitch."

She couldn't really move because the scuba diver had her legs wrapped around her head with his arms. You can guess where the rest of him was.

No one said anything as he slowly untangled all the limbs. I kept blinking my eyes, trying to comprehend.

"Oh, hell," I saw her whisper, once freed, as she rolled toward the bulkhead.

All I heard from him was a mumble, as he hurriedly pulled on his bikini. I admired his aplomb.

Then the three of us remained still, with only the sound of the water lapping the sides of the boat to interrupt the silence. I was the first to move. I sank to the top of the stair—causing scuba boy to jump, bumping his head against the ceiling.

Then I heard myself ask, "Where is *She*?" And there was no reply.

"Where *is* She, you cocksucker?" I demanded, half standing.

Janet moaned, turning completely toward the wall.

"Look," the scuba diver said quietly, "if you'll just keep calm, this whole thing's going to work out all right."

"Work out!" I screamed, knowing the sound pained him. "Where is *She*? Where the hell is *she*?"

"She . . . she isn't here," he replied tentatively.

"I saw you pick Her up," I said. "I saw you leave the harbor in Freeport. And I want to know where She is."

"Oh, God," Janet moaned, the sound of tears mixing in.

Again all three of us remained silent, fixed, as it were, in a vacuum.

That's when I saw it—scattered all over the bed, part of the softness, the luxury. At first I had to squint to try to decipher. But then it became clearer and clearer. It was all there. The shawl. The long full-flowered dress. Even the wig. A round, gray wig. Just as I had seen in Freeport. Janet's arm lay across it.

"Look," the scuba diver said, his voice trembling momentarily, "you've got the money. Just go home. Don't ask any questions. Don't fuck everything up."

I couldn't speak, but I could think. Something was confirmed, but I didn't know what. I had to wait. I looked at Janet, her perfection sprawled amidst the seedy old clothes. It couldn't have been. But apparently it was.

"From the beginning?" I said to Janet. There was no reply.

"How is that possible?" I asked, wanting to touch her, because I somehow knew I never would again.

"Oh, you jerk," she said, not moving her head. "Do the smart thing."

"The what?" I whispered. "The *what*? Make me smart. Tell me the truth! Where is She! Are you *Her*!"

And then came the sound—the godawful shriek I had first heard over a year before—a lifetime before—"Yes, child, it's the Godmother. You will do what you're told. You will be a good boy."

Stunned—no, paralyzed—I looked toward her head. But nothing had changed. The sound had come from somewhere else. I turned toward the door and saw nothing. There were only the three of us. I had only one place to turn. I turned toward . . . him.

"That's right, asshole," he said, his voice modulating in mock of the Godmother. "You finally wised up. And let me tell you something else. This lady is mine—"

"Wait a minute!" I gasped. "Wait a minute! Are *you* the Godmother?"

Janet groaned once again and sat up. "Oh, Bob, you silly ass! We're *both* the Godmother. Just let it drop. Take your damned money and get lost. The game's over. Just get lost."

"But how . . . how did you get the figures?" I asked, still not able to believe what I was hearing.

"I ran the security program for the money supply at the Treasury," he smirked. "How could I run the program without gaining access to the information? My only problem was I had to set up safeguards against myself. That meant I had to have help. You were it. Thank you, Bob. Now get out."

"But what about the painter?" I asked Janet, realizing the indiscretion.

"There was no painter," she replied with fatigue. "You're looking at him."

"But what are you doing down here teaching scuba diving?" I asked.

"I resigned several weeks ago," he replied with impatience. "This was as good a cover as any to collect the money."

I stared first at him, then at her. I then watched him lean over and open a cabinet. He casually produced a pistol and pointed it toward me.

"I spent time in Vietnam before the Secret Service," he announced. "I know how to use this. I know how to kill. Take your money and leave, right now. And keep your fucking mouth shut. Forever."

The pistol got my attention. And it was quite clear Janet wasn't going with me. And, frankly, I didn't care. It seemed my whole life was over. There was nothing left to hope for.

I climbed the stairs, emerging into the dazzling sunlight. He followed behind, holding the pistol behind his back.

"You don't know what you've done," I said.

"Get off the boat," he growled, switching on the bilge gas blowers to vent gasoline fumes prior to starting the engine.

"It's not just Janet," I said, throwing my leg over the side and tossing the satchel to the dock. "It's *Her* too. The Godmother. It's almost as if you've destroyed Her."

"So long, Bob," he said, descending once again to the cabin. "Have a nice life."

I stood with one leg hanging over the rail. I decided suddenly to try one more time—to try to recover, somehow, my lost vision. I returned to the deck and walked to the helm station. I turned *off* the bilge gas blowers. They couldn't leave, now. They couldn't take the Godmother with them!

Almost immediately he jumped out of the cabin, not even bothering to hide the pistol.

"You get off this fucking boat, or I'll blow your head off!" he shouted. "We're leaving right now. You'll never see us again. Got that straight?"

I stumbled backward and struggled ashore. I picked up the satchel and turned back toward the boat.

"You can't do this to another human being!" I shouted, as he fumbled with the dials. "It's not right! It's not . . . fair!"

He didn't bother to reply. He simply reached toward the ignition button and pushed it. I could hear the engines begin to whine, as I felt myself fall toward the wooden planking of the dock. And then, some time later, I remember an enormous explosion and the rush of air and bits above me. And then there was nothing but the sound of objects dropping into the sea. One by one. Monotonously. And I knew She was gone. There was nothing left.

I stood and walked away. And I never looked back.

Charles Baxter Clement is a graduate of Princeton and the University of Virginia Law School. After an extensive business career in Europe, Africa, and the Middle East, he formed a prominent brokerage and trading operation at the Chicago Board of Trade. This is his first novel.